REDACTION

RACHEL HATCH
BOOK 12

L.T. RYAN

with

BRIAN SHEA

LIQUID MIND MEDIA

For information contact:

contact@ltryan.com

http://LTRyan.com

https://www.facebook.com/JackNobleBooks

THE RACHEL HATCH SERIES

Drift

Downburst

Fever Burn

Smoke Signal

Firewalk

Whitewater

Aftershock

Whirlwind

Tsunami

Fastrope

Sidewinder

Redaction

Mirage

RACHEL HATCH SHORT STORIES

Fractured

Proving Ground

The Gauntlet

Join the LT Ryan reader family & receive a free copy of the Rachel Hatch story, Fractured. Click the link below to get started:

https://ltryan.com/rachel-hatch-newsletter-signup-1

Love Hatch? Noble? Maddie? Cassie? Get your very own Jack Noble merchandise today! Click the link below to find coffee mugs, t-shirts, and even signed copies of your favorite L.T. Ryan thrillers! https://ltryan.ink/EvG_

ONE

RAIN HAMMERED DOWN ON MALCOLM TRENT, ICY NAILS, RELENTLESS AND cold, penetrating through his coat down to his bones. Water filled his boots. Evening had passed to early night, the light transitioning from gray to black without so much as a flicker of sunset. His headlamp did little for his eyesight in these conditions. The hours spent battling the rising floodwater from the stream left him exhausted, sweat adding its brine to the mix. An early spring thaw, coupled with torrential rain, threatened to erode his land, making planting season a more arduous task than it already was.

Every sandbag he set was quickly overcome by the waterline. It was a man versus mother nature battle royale, and she was setting him up for the knockout. He set the last of his sandbags on the stack lining the bend. His legs trembled and his back ached. There was a time when he could've kept pace for another couple of hours. Those days had long since passed. He let out a low groan as he stretched before turning his back to the rushing water.

Smoke seeped from the chimney of his ranch. He was glad to see the fire was still burning. He began his trek up the muddy landscape, his boots sinking to the heel with each step. Malcom passed by his well. Over the rattling of its tin roof, he heard the roar of engines.

Two black SUVs rolled up the gravel driveway, their tires slipping against the slick, loose stones. The polished vehicles gleamed under the wet assault. He continued to his house and climbed the steps leading to his door. He didn't get many visitors. Definitely not on a night like this. He took a step towards his shotgun, leaning against the porch railing.

The sight of those sleek cars and the man in the front passenger seat of the second vehicle churned his stomach.

He reached for the shotgun, lifted it off the railing, and fired into the air. The sharp report cut through the storm. He was beyond pleasantries.

The well-dressed man leading the group emerged with an umbrella held over his head, his features impassive, as if the gunshot warning barely registered. His associates flanked him, silent, their movements precise.

"Mr. Trent," the man called, his voice a smooth blade slicing through the rain. "I'm afraid we still have some unfinished business."

The umbrella man's cohort adjusted his coat, revealing the holstered pistol at his side, an understated but clear message. Compliance wasn't optional.

"I already told you. I'm not selling." Malcolm lowered the shotgun slightly but kept his grip firm on the stock. "There's nothing left to talk about, Mr. Covington. Best you and your friends be goin' now. Before I decide to be less hospitable with my point of aim."

"You sure are a stubborn old coot." No humor in the man's voice, the coldness with which he spoke matched the rain's relentless assault. "Unfortunately, the terms are non-negotiable." He gestured toward the house. "Shall we?"

The two men behind him took a step forward, outnumbering Malcom, outgunning him. He wanted to resist, to take a stand for the land that had been in his family for generations. But what could he do against this kind of power?

Malcolm cursed and turned toward the house, his hands tightening on the shotgun as he led the way. The conversation that was about to take place would change everything.

"Mr. Trent, be a dear and leave that shotgun out here."

Malcom hesitated, keeping his grip tight on the gun, before doing as he was told. Once inside, the warmth of his living room felt like a betrayal. Beauregard Covington set his umbrella alongside the shotgun and sauntered in. He directed Malcom to sit.

Covington took a handkerchief from his breast pocket and wiped off a spot on the threadbare couch, placing a briefcase between them like an executioner laying down his tools. His eyes locked with Malcolm's. "The future of this property isn't something you can afford to decide on sentiment alone, Mr. Trent. This is business. And I am a businessman."

"You're nothing of the sort. You've been chasing people off their property." Malcolm's teeth clenched, sending a ripple along his jaw. "You're nothing but a two-bit thug. And I got the right mind to—"

Covington held up a finger, bringing silence to the room. Any hint of the false charm was gone. "This back and forth has become tiresome. It seems to me we are at an impasse. Would you agree?"

Malcom stalled. His eyes darted around to the other men in the room. The walls were closing in. A tremor vibrated his gaunt frame. It wasn't the soaking clothes clinging to him. It was the coldness in the man across from him that unsettled Malcom to his core.

"Then I guess you leave me no choice." Covington signaled to a man standing behind him.

Before Malcom could turn to face this unseen threat, he was struck at the base of his skull. Pain radiated in his head and spread throughout his body. The warm light cast by his fireplace was immediately doused. The last thing he saw was the bright white of Covington's suit before it was exchanged for darkness.

THE ICY WATER continued its slow, relentless crawl up Malcolm Trent's legs, a creeping reminder of the end that was fast approaching. Suspended by ropes tied to his wrists, Malcolm's body hung limp, exhaustion and cold rendering him numb to the biting pain. The world had narrowed to the sound of water rushing through the stone walls of the well and the quiet creak of the ropes as they strained to hold his weight. Each passing second drained more of the fight from him.

His mind, once sharp, was now fogged by the cold, drifting between flashes of regret and memories that felt too far away. Even the throbbing ache in his wrists had dulled. Only the rising water remained as the one thing he could still feel, its presence inescapable as it slowly claimed him. The melted snow and spring rains had conspired to make the well a death trap.

This was not the way he'd expected to die, alone in the dark, hanging above the very water that had once sustained his family's land. Malcolm had fought his entire life for that land. He'd worked this land since his childhood, following in his father's footsteps. Down the line it had gone for nearly two hundred years. And now, as the floodwaters slowly rose, he was to be buried with it.

He tried to picture his daughter, Maggie. The guilt gnawed at him; they hadn't spoken in years. Stubbornness had cost him so much more than he was willing to admit. Now, all he wanted was forgiveness for the harsh words he'd spoken at her mother's funeral. Words that had driven his daughter away when he'd needed her most.

As the water touched his chest, Malcolm gasped for breath, his lungs burning with the cold. The darkness was closing in, his vision tunneling. A warmth, strange in this cold place, settled over him. Was this how it felt to die? He thought of Glenda, his late wife. He had failed her. To his daughter, his firefly. He had failed them both.

Against his will, his head dropped, chin resting against his collarbone. His eyes closed as he surrendered to the inevitable. The Trent family legacy was ending here, in the cold, unfeeling ground.

Then, his thoughts stilled, and all that was left was the sound of the gurgling water.

TWO

THE SOFT SAND OF CORONADO BEACH SHIFTED BENEATH HATCH'S FEET AS she ran along the shoreline, the rhythmic crashing of waves mirroring the steady cadence of her breathing. Early morning mist clung to the horizon, shrouding the Silver Strand Highway in a thin veil while the ocean air carried the crisp saltiness she'd grown to associate with this stretch of California coast.

As Hatch slowed her pace, sweat cooling against her skin, she turned her attention to the water. A group of BUD/S trainees struggled to push their rigid inflatable boats through the relentless breakers, the waves towering over them in their furious attempts to surge forward. The boats pitched and rolled, the students straining as they heaved against the ocean's might, fighting for every inch.

She watched them with an expression somewhere between admiration and melancholy, reminded of the man who'd once navigated those same waters with effortless grace.

A gust of wind swept in from the sea, tangling her hair in the salty breeze, and in that moment, Cruise's memory enveloped her. It wasn't just the salty air that brought him back—it was something more, something in the way the breeze curled against her, like it carried a part of him within it. She could almost smell him in the air, that scent of salt-water and sun-kissed skin. The ocean had always been a part of Cruise, and now he was a part of it—forever intertwined with the endless tides.

Hatch pulled her focus away from the struggling trainees, her breath catching as the bittersweet memory tugged at her. She glanced down at the shifting sand beneath her feet, grounding herself in the present, but the weight of the past lingered in the air, as constant and vast as the ocean stretching before her.

She closed her eyes, just for a moment, feeling the pull of the sea and the man who had become part of it. Then, with a deep breath, she opened them again, refocusing on the horizon. The waves crashed, the world moved on, and so would she—though part of her would always remain here, on the edge of the water, chasing memories of a man lost to the sea.

Hatch's phone vibrated against her hip. Grateful for the distraction, she slowed her pace and pulled it from the small fanny pack around her waist. The screen lit up with Tracy's name.

"Good morning," she greeted, her voice carrying the edge of ragged breath as her heart rate began to settle.

"Not sure how good it is." Tracy's voice had a sharpness to it, a tension she wasn't used to hearing from him. "Need you to come in."

"Everything alright?" Hatch asked, wiping a hand across her damp forehead, though the cooling ocean breeze did little to ease the sudden knot of worry forming in her gut.

"We'll see. I'll get you up to speed when you get here. How far out are you?"

Hatch glanced at her surroundings, the iconic red roof of the Hotel Del Coronado just ahead. "By Hotel Del. Do I have time to rinse off?"

"This is a come-as-you-are powwow," he replied, the words heavy with meaning, void of any humor.

"Be there in fifteen." She paused, the weight of his mood pressing down on her. "Anything else I should know?"

"Brace for impact." With that, the line went dead.

Hatch exhaled slowly, lowering the phone. She cast a fleeting glance back at the struggling BUD/S trainees in the surf, catching sight of the lead boat capsizing as the giant wave rolled over them, scattering the occupants toward shore.

Whatever was coming her way, she had the sinking suspicion she'd rather be in that boat, fighting the current.

––––––––––

HATCH SAT in the conference room, her back ramrod straight as tension coiled in her shoulders. The room was nondescript to the point of irritation—beige walls, a scuffed table, and fluorescent lights that hummed like a persistent mosquito. For someone who thrived in chaos, she found the sterile monotony unnerving. Her eyes locked onto the unfamiliar face at the head of the table, taking in every detail: the sharp jawline, the calculated movements, the way his eyes swept the room like a predator sizing up its prey.

Jordan Tracy sat to her right, his usual calm unraveling with each second that ticked by. He tapped a pen against the edge of his notepad, the rhythmic click echoing in the quiet room. Hatch shot him a sidelong glance, noting the tightness in his jaw and the slight sheen of sweat on his temple.

To her left, Ed Banyan sprawled in his chair, one arm draped lazily over the backrest. But Hatch wasn't fooled by his nonchalance; his fingers drummed against his thigh in a restless cadence, and his eyes darted to the door as if gauging the quickest escape route.

Hatch shifted in her chair, the cheap vinyl creaking beneath her. The scent of stale coffee and industrial cleaner hung in the air, mixing with the undercurrent of unspoken tension. She rested her palms flat on the table, forcing herself to remain still despite the urge to match Tracy's nervous energy.

"Hatch," the man at the head of the table began, his voice stern and commanding. "I'm William Thorne."

"Sir." Hatch gave a curt nod. Tracy had been less than forthcoming as to the nature of the meeting. Reading his body language spoke volumes.

"We've never had the pleasure of meeting. That's a good thing. Cut my teeth in the Army, finishing my time as a Brigadier General with SOCOM. I'm in charge of asset management and operational oversight here at Talon Executive Services."

Great. Internal Affairs. In Hatch's past life, it was never good when called to the carpet. From the look on the general's face, this was not the exception.

"We're here to discuss your recent *activities* in Diamondback, Arizona."

"Understood."

Thorne leaned back in his chair, fingers steepled as he assessed her. "Walk me through it."

Hatch let out a slow exhale. "We were in Diamondback to assist in gathering information for Max Carver."

"When you say *we*, you're referring to you and Banyan, correct?"

"Correct."

"Explain to me why two Talon assets were conducting an unsanctioned operation without proper approval."

"General, I've already explained this was done as a personal favor to me." Tracy sat forward. "Max and I go way back. This was supposed to be a simple fact-finding mission. Nothing more."

"But it became something more. Much more. Wouldn't you agree?" Thorne shifted his attention back to Hatch. "Now, I'd like to better understand how this situation escalated so far out of control."

Hatch spent the next several minutes recounting her time in Arizona. She discussed the rapid escalation. Carver's client, Harvey Linden, had been targeted by a dangerous group of Belarusian mobsters. That Linden's family was in imminent harm and the wife had been kidnapped.

Anger flashed behind Thorne's eyes. His hands pressed hard into the desk between them as he stood. "This little stunt could've compromised the agency. We operate behind the scenes. We get tapped to handle the types of jobs others are incapable of. We aren't the A-Team, out there looking for trouble. We are the problem solvers, not creators. Get me?"

"In Hatch's defense," Banyan said, "she freed the hostages. We dismantled the Novik family's entire operation, rescuing Linden's children as well."

Thorne shook his head, unimpressed. "You had other options. Options that didn't involve a major incident that could have compromised the integrity of Talon."

A spark of defiance flared in Hatch's chest. "With all due respect, sir, when good people's lives are on the line, standing idly by is not an option for me. Especially when I know I can handle saving them."

Tracy tried to interject on her behalf once more, but Thorne silenced him with a single look. Banyan, ever the provocateur, chimed in casually. "General, maybe it's been too long since you strapped on your own combat boots and gone toe to toe with the enemy."

"You're on thin ice. I wouldn't push too much or you might fall in." Thorne's eyes narrowed. "I'd hate to see you lose that new assignment you put in for."

Hatch shot Banyan a questioning look. He refused to meet her eyes.

Tracy's unease was apparent. The man wasn't known for timidity, but even he seemed wary of the situation unraveling further.

"I'm not a man who gives second chances. All of you are put on notice." Thorne turned his focus back to Hatch. "Your next assignment will be your last if you can't play by the rules." He straightened his tie and walked out without another word to any of them.

The three of them lingered in the room, ensuring the general was gone before making their exit. As they filed out, Hatch muttered to Tracy, "What the hell was that all about? Seems like he's on a witch hunt."

Tracy sighed. "General Thorne was a hell of a soldier back in the day, Hatch. But the politics of rank have a way of diluting that."

"Guess so. It just seemed personal. Like he's gunning for us. For me."

"Don't overthink it. Everybody in our line of work gets our pee pee slapped from time to time." Tracy smirked. "It's how you know you're doing something right."

Hatch pulled on Banyan's elbow. "Hey, what was that back there? The talk about a new assignment?"

Banyan rubbed a hand on the back of his neck. "I was going to let you know. Haven't had the chance."

"I'll give you guys a chance to get up to speed." Tracy nodded and moved toward the door.

"How 'bout we grab a coffee?" Banyan asked.

"You ever heard me turning down a cup?"

THREE

Hatch stepped into the quiet café. The comforting smell of freshly brewed coffee mingled with the soft murmur of morning conversations. Sunlight filtered through the windows, casting warm streaks across the tables. She spotted Banyan sitting in the back, near the window, casually sipping his coffee.

"My treat," Banyan said, sliding a cup of coffee across the table as Hatch approached.

She sat down, letting the warmth of the café envelop her. The muted hum of conversation and the faint hiss of the espresso machine filled the air, a welcome contrast to the sharp tension that seemed to cling to Banyan. Hatch wrapped her hands around the ceramic mug, savoring the heat that seeped into her palms.

Banyan leaned back in his chair with a sigh, his usually easygoing demeanor replaced by something heavier. His gaze lingered on the tabletop, the furrow in his brow deepening. Hatch took a sip, her eyes never leaving him as she waited for him to speak.

She studied Banyan's averted gaze. "Still figuring out what you have to tell me?"

Banyan leaned forward, his usual grin replaced by something far more solemn. "Figured it best to deal with all the stuff with Thorne first. This … this is more of a 'coffee-shop confession' kind of thing."

Hatch raised an eyebrow. "You're dancing around something. Out with it."

Taking a slow breath, his eyes shifted to the window before locking back onto hers. "I've been offered a new role. Head of advanced technologies at Talon."

Hatch's brow furrowed. "Advanced technologies? What exactly is that?"

"It's something I pitched to them after Omnisphere. The listening device system we test ran in Arizona."

"You mean the unauthorized test run," she corrected.

He offered a shrug of indifference. "Either way. The brass got wind and apparently liked what they saw. They asked me if I wanted a change of pace."

Hatch studied him, sensing something deeper beneath the words. "Change of pace how?"

"No more fieldwork," Banyan said, stirring sugar into his coffee. "I'll be a regular nine-to-five kind of guy."

"Please tell me you're not going to start wearing a suit and tie?"

"Never. Board shorts and flip-flops for life." His smile didn't quite reach his eyes.

"Why didn't you tell me sooner?"

"I wasn't sure I wanted it, to be honest. Didn't want to leave you out there all alone."

Hatch leaned back. "I'm a big girl."

Banyan hesitated. "I know. It's just—"

"Seriously, don't give it another thought. You've gotta do what's right for you. And remember, I'm the one who wanted to work alone, anyway." She shrugged. "Guess now it's official."

Banyan's grin returned, softer now. "I'll always have your back. Just a phone call away."

"You're going to be like Q from the Bond movies now."

"Guess that makes you 007."

"Hatch. Rachel Hatch," she said, putting on her best Sean Connery impression.

Banyan chuckled, but the lightness faded seconds later.

"You're a good operator. You sure Talon won't miss you out here?"

"*I'll* miss it, for sure," he admitted after a beat. "But I've been thinking a lot about my family. It's time to stop putting them on the back burner."

Hatch understood the pull of family all too well. The weight of responsibility to others had a way of shifting priorities.

Banyan reached into his jacket pocket. "Got something for you." He set a small, matte-black case on the table between them.

Hatch raised an eyebrow. "What's that? A retirement gift?"

"Something like that." Banyan flipped the case open to reveal a small, circular patch. "This, my friend, is the future."

Hatch gingerly picked up the patch, turning it over in her hand. It felt smooth and rubbery. "What does it do?"

Banyan leaned in slightly, his voice dropping. "It's a modern-day cyanide pill. Inside that patch is a tiny ampule. Press it, it breaks, and it releases a chemical that slows your heartbeat to undetectable levels. For all intents and purposes, you appear dead."

"Dead?" Hatch raised her brow. "And then what?"

"It wears off after about ten minutes. Enough time for the bad guys to move on and for you to make your escape."

Hatch stared at the patch, considering its potential. "Playing possum was never my thing," she muttered. After a pause, she added, "But ... how's it work exactly?"

Banyan's eyes lit up with the enthusiasm of an engineer explaining his masterpiece. "The patch contains a bradycardic agent—a synthetic version of the venom from the blue-ringed octopus. It dramatically slows your heart rate and respiration, just like the venom does."

Hatch smirked. "Octopus venom? You've gotta be kidding."

"Dead serious," Banyan replied, his voice dipping back into the solemn tone. "It mimics death. Drops the pulse to an undetectable level. Blood circulates just enough oxygen to keep a person alive. Combine that with a vasodilator to lower blood pressure further, and you're clinically dead, as far as anyone else can tell."

She studied the patch a little more closely. "And how do you come back?"

"A time-release antidote kicks in after ten minutes, restoring your heart rate and blood pressure. I'm still working on increasing the time between doses, but that's the best I've got right now."

Hatch let the information settle. The soft clatter of cups and the low hum of conversation provided a fragile sense of normalcy, at odds with their world. "Is it safe?"

Banyan's face grew serious. "It's not without risks. The dosage is calibrated for your specific weight and physiology, but there's always a chance of an adverse reaction."

Hatch set the patch back in the case, snapping it shut. "But it's been tested?"

"Extensively," Banyan said. "On animals and controlled human trials. It's ready for the field."

She pushed the case back across the table, but Banyan stopped it halfway, nudging it back toward her. "Consider it a parting gift."

She hesitated, then thought more on it. First rule of preparedness: Better to have it and not need it, than to need it and not have it. She pocketed the case. "I guess you can never be too prepared."

"With you, that's the understatement of the century." Banyan raised his cup in a toast. "Here's to playing dead."

Hatch clinked her mug to his. "And to coming back to life."

Her phone rattled against the tabletop as she took a swig. It was Tracy again. Hatch answered.

"You're up," he said. "Op just came in. Solo."

"I'm sure the General will be happy about that."

"Order came from him."

Hatch furrowed her brow and downed the remainer of her coffee. "You think it's a test?"

"Maybe. He's a hard man to read. Could be a way of saying water under the bridge."

"Or putting me out to pasture."

"Looks like a softball contract. You're just adding some extra muscle to a protective detail," Tracy said. "Wheels up in an hour. Grab your gear. I'll meet you at the hangar and give you a full brief."

Hatch glanced at Banyan, who raised an eyebrow, clearly picking up on the change in her demeanor. "See you then."

"And Hatch..." Tracy paused. "Dress warm. You're heading to New Hampshire."

The line went dead. Hatch set the phone down, her fingers tapping lightly against the screen, the weight of the call lingering.

Banyan had an expectant look. "Everything alright?"

Hatch exhaled slowly. "Guess we'll find out."

FOUR

EVELYN HARTWELL STEPPED OUT OF THE LOCAL GROCERY STORE NESTLED in the heart of Pinewood Falls. The picturesque New Hampshire town, with its mom-and-pop shops lining the main street, was a postcard of serenity—at least on the surface. Evelyn balanced grocery bags in her arms, while her twelve-year-old daughter Chloe followed closely behind, bundled in a puffer jacket to ward off the crisp air.

"Let me help you with those bags." Tommy, the young grocery bagger, stepped outside behind them.

"That's very kind of you, Tommy, but we can manage. Thank you."

They made their way down the sidewalk, the sounds of small-town life surrounding them—the distant laughter of children in the park, the comforting scent of fresh bread wafting from the bakery, and the crunch of fallen leaves beneath their winter boots. Pinewood Falls felt like a place frozen in time, but Evelyn's world was far from peaceful. Beneath her calm exterior, worry gnawed at her, refusing to let go.

Chloe tugged at her sleeve. "Mom, we need to stop by the pharmacy. I'm almost out of my medicine."

Evelyn's cheeks warmed. Her mind had been in a thousand places, aside from where it needed to be. "Of course. I can't believe I almost forgot."

"That's why you've got me." Chloe wore a proud smile. "To help keep things straight."

"Don't know what I'd do without you." She laid a kiss on the top of her daughter's head.

Entering the pharmacy, the familiar jingle of the bell above the door offered a moment of comfort. Mr. Jameson, the kind-hearted pharmacist, looked up from behind the counter.

"Evelyn, Chloe! Always good to see you both. How can I help today?"

Evelyn handed over the prescription, her fingers trembling slightly. Mr. Jameson took the slip, disappearing behind the counter to process the order.

Chloe leaned against the counter, her body language betraying her exhaustion. Evelyn's eyes darted between her daughter and Mr. Jameson, the pressure of everything—Chloe's health, the bills, the endless struggle to stay afloat—tightening her chest.

A few minutes later, Mr. Jameson returned, his expression less cheerful, more apologetic. "I hate to tell you this, but it looks like your insurance has lapsed. I tried applying a discount code for you, but the best I could do is $150 out of pocket."

Evelyn's stomach dropped, her voice barely above a whisper. "My insurance ... I couldn't afford to renew the plan Kevin had before he passed. I'm trying to get full-time status at the vet clinic, but until then ... no benefits."

Mr. Jameson sighed, clearly feeling for her. He glanced at Chloe, whose pale face reflected her need. He softened his tone. "I know things have been tough, Evelyn. Pay what you can for now. We'll figure the rest out later."

Evelyn's heart ached with gratitude, but shame crept in just as quickly. Reaching into her purse, she pulled out the little cash she had, barely enough to make a dent. "Thank you," she murmured, her voice tight with emotion. "I'll pay more as soon as I can."

Mr. Jameson placed a comforting hand on her shoulder. "You're not alone in this. We'll make sure Chloe gets what she needs."

Tears threatened to spill from her eyes. Evelyn blinked them away. One escaped her lashes, and she was quick to wipe it before Chloe saw.

With the medicine in hand, they stepped out of the pharmacy. It was colder now than before they'd entered the warm building.

As they made their way toward their station wagon, a familiar voice called out. "Ms. Hartwell!"

Evelyn turned to see Liam, a teenager with unruly red hair, jogging toward them, a stack of flyers in his hand. His earnest expression made him look even younger than he was, a beacon of the town's hopeful youth.

"Would you be interested in attending the rally tomorrow?" Liam asked, slightly out of breath. "We're protesting the corporate takeover of our town's natural resources."

Evelyn allowed a playfulness to her tone. "Does your father know you're out here stirring up trouble?"

"He's doing his part to keep people safe." Liam shrugged. "I'm doing mine."

Chloe took one of the flyers, her pale cheeks flushing with a spark of excitement. "Are you going to the rally?"

"Wouldn't miss it, kiddo," Liam said, ruffling her hair. "Maybe you can convince your mom to come."

Evelyn met her husband years back when she was a waitress at a truck stop. He was a long-haul driver. It wasn't a Romeo and Juliet star-crossed lover's fairytale, but it was their story. The byproduct of their love was the daughter that they made together. Her husband's death had left a hole in both their lives.

Small town life meant everyone knew each other's business. The community had been supportive in the wake of his death, but it was Liam who seemed to be able to bring out the kid in her daughter. The son of the town's sheriff, the teenager was as trustworthy as they came. He'd been Chloe's babysitter, but after she was diagnosed with Type 1 diabetes, he took on the role of surrogate big brother. The way Chloe lit up every time he was around filled her with joy.

But her happiness was dashed at the sight of a sleek black Cadillac Escalade parked alongside her car.

"Time to go, honey." She instinctually reached down and grabbed her daughter's hand, giving it a slight squeeze. "Bye Liam."

"Think about it!" The boy said as the pair swiftly walked toward her car.

Her grip tightened on Chloe's hand as Beauregard Covington stepped out of the SUV, his white suit a stark contrast to the rustic surroundings. He approached with a slow, calculated stride.

"Mrs. Hartwell," Covington drawled, his voice smooth and sickly sweet. "I believe we have some unfinished business."

Evelyn's pulse quickened as she tried to step around him, but one of Covington's men blocked her path. Chloe pressed in closer, seeming to sense her tension.

"How many different ways do you need me to say it? I won't sign." Evelyn fought to control the tremble in her voice. "This is our home. I won't let you take it."

"Many of your fellow townsfolk said the very same thing. All of them came to their senses. All of them but you."

"You forgot Malcom Trent?"

"Didn't you hear?" Covington's teeth gleamed, matching the brightness of his suit. A cold amusement danced across his face. "Mr. Trent saw things differently. He came to his senses last night. Signed the papers. Now there's only you."

Evelyn's heart skipped a beat. "No... Malcolm would never—"

"But he did," Covington purred. He pulled out a document from inside the breast pocket of his suitcoat.

Evelyn stepped close enough to see Malcolm Trent's signature scrawled at the bottom. She also noticed a dark, rust-colored stain beside it, which spoke volumes as to how that had come to pass. "Now, I suggest you follow suit. No need to draw out the inevitable."

"You don't scare me," she said, hoping her fear didn't break the surface.

"You seem like a good mother. Don't you want your daughter to get the best care possible? Give her a better life. Better than the one you're currently giving her."

Chloe broke free of her mom's grasp and stepped forward with her fists balled. "You don't know anything. My life's perfect. My mom's the best in the whole world!"

Convington chuckled softly and stooped to meet the little girl's defiant eyes. "I'm sure she is. But I'm not sure you'd be singing the same tune if you lost your house and were out on the streets."

Evelyn caught Chloe by her sleeve before her daughter took a step closer. "Don't ever speak to my daughter. You address me and me alone." Rage burned inside. A fire she hadn't felt in a long time, if ever.

Before the moment could erupt into something worse, Liam stepped in. "You should leave, Mr. Covington. My father's the sheriff. He won't stand for you harassing Ms. Hartwell."

For a moment, Covington didn't move a muscle. He quietly considered the boy. "No need for unpleasantness, young man. This is just business."

Cold rain began to fall from the dark clouds above. Nobody moved. Nobody crossed the invisible line between them.

Covington let out a loud sigh. Looking past Liam, he locked eyes on Evelyn. "I'll be by in a day or two. Hopefully, it'll be enough time for you to reconsider. After that, the terms won't be so friendly."

His words lingered, the threat behind them unmistakable. Covington turned and strode back to his SUV. His men followed without a word, leaving Evelyn standing there, shaken.

Liam touched her arm gently. "Ms. Hartwell, if you need anything—anything at all—my dad and I are here for you."

"Thanks, Liam. Means more than you know." Her mind raced. She was the last holdout, the only person standing between the town and Crystal Springs. She wasn't sure she could stand her ground much longer. She looked down at Chloe. The image of the rust-colored stain on Trent's deed flashed in her mind's eye.

They got into the car, blasting the heat to max, and drove away. The flyer for the rally fluttered on the dashboard, a quiet reminder of the battle yet to come.

FIVE

THE HANGAR STRETCHED OUT LIKE A STEEL CATHEDRAL, COLD AND industrial. Fluorescent lights buzzed overhead, their sharp glare bouncing off the polished concrete ground. The cavernous space amplified every sound—the distant clang of tools against metal, the low hum of maintenance carts moving along the edges, and the faint echo of voices calling out instructions. The air was heavy with the scent of jet fuel and the faint metallic tang of grease. Hatch's boots barely made a sound as she moved across the vast space, her eyes taking in every detail.

At the far end, a Gulfstream G550 sat, sleek and deadly. Its pristine silver body gleamed under the artificial lights, every angle designed for efficiency and dominance. The cockpit windows glinted like the eyes of a predator, and the faint vibration from its engines hinted at the raw power waiting beneath its sleek exterior. Hatch could smell the familiar blend of jet fuel, engine oil, and rubber from the stacked Goodyear tires nearby. It was the smell of readiness, precision.

Tracy's voice cut through the quiet. "Ready for this?"

Hatch slowed her walk and flicked her gaze over to him. He stood next to a heavy-duty Pelican case, an encrypted digital tablet in hand, his casual posture betrayed by the tension in his shoulders. There was always tension with Tracy, and the fact that she still didn't know the full scope of the mission didn't help.

It wasn't like him to hold back details this late in the game. She wondered if it was strategic or if he was just unsure about what they were walking into. Either way, it grated on her nerves to be in the dark.

"Hard to be ready when I'm flying blind," she shot back, her voice dry.

Tracy handed over a file, the paper inside crisp and freshly printed. "You're on asset protection. Senator Masterson, New Hampshire. He's up for re-election and is concerned about his safety after a leaked campaign donation from Crystal Springs."

"Heard of them." Hatch flipped through the file. "Most of it not good. The media's been hammering them. Claims of small-town buyouts for profit."

She'd read enough to know how companies like Crystal Springs operated—faceless money machines swallowing communities whole while politicians lined their pockets with the aftermath. Masterson might well be just another cog in their assembly line of greed.

"Apparently they're putting some of those profits into backing political candidates." Tracy crossed his arms. "One happens to be Masterson. It's caused him a bit of trouble."

"What kind of trouble?"

"He's been getting death threats. The list of potential suspects is endless. Environmental groups are after him, pissed-off locals, and so on. Nothing specific, but Masterson's security isn't taking any chances."

"Sounds like he's in bed with the wrong people." Hatch continued scrolling the page. "Why am I involved if he's already got a security team?"

"We're providing an additional asset to ease the senator's worry. And that happens to be you." Tracy passed her a dossier. "Your point of contact is Ethan Reeves. Head of security, ex-military. Solid record. You'll be in good hands."

Of course, it wasn't just about security. It never was. If Thorne was involved, there were layers she wasn't seeing yet—layers that would probably surface when it was too late to do anything about them.

Hatch lifted her gaze to meet Tracy's. "Seems like overkill."

"Masterson's a close friend of Thorne's. The General offered up Talon's services as a personal favor."

Hatch snorted, a sharp laugh escaping her. "So now the general's pimping us out for personal favors? Funny, considering he chewed my ass out for doing the same for you."

"I get it. But this is an opportunity to clear things with Thorne. Get back in his good graces." Tracy rubbed the back of his neck.

Hatch knew better than to trust easy missions or empty promises of reconciliation. People like Thorne didn't forget or forgive—they calculated. This felt less like redemption and more like being maneuvered into position for the next move on the chessboard.

"Easy op. You go in, keep an eye on the senator, and get out. No complications."

"Things can get complicated all by themselves," Hatch muttered. "And if that happens, is the general going to have my back or hang me out to dry?"

"Let's hope we don't have to find out."

"What's the timeline on this babysitting assignment?"

"Just a day. Two at most," Tracy said. "Masterson has a town hall meeting tomorrow. Once that's done, he's back on the campaign trail, and you're back at base."

"Sounds easy enough."

"Play nice, and maybe we'll get off Thorne's shit list."

Hatch turned and headed toward the Gulfstream, the morning sun catching the polished metal as she climbed the narrow staircase.

This wasn't the kind of assignment she'd signed up for when she joined Talon, but maybe that was the point. You don't get to pick and choose in this world—you take the orders, do the job, and hope you can live with yourself afterward.

Inside, the cabin was everything she expected—dark leather seats, polished wood accents, and enough tech embedded in the walls to run a small-scale operation from the air. The air smelled faintly of leather and disinfectant, a sterile kind of luxury. The ambient hum of the aircraft's systems provided a low, constant background noise, and the recessed lighting cast soft pools of light across the cabin's gleaming surfaces. Everything about it screamed wealth and efficiency—tools of power wrapped in comfort.

Dropping into one of the plush seats, Hatch opened the file again. Senator Masterson's grinning face stared back at her, his eyes filled with the kind of arrogance that only came from years of politics and corporate handshakes.

The Gulfstream's engines roared to life as they taxied out of the hangar. The aircraft glided forward, its tires rumbling softly over the hangar's concrete floor. Outside the window, the landscape blurred into motion—metal scaffolding, fuel trucks, and distant runways disappearing as they approached the open sky.

SIX

THE MOUNTAIN VIEW DINER WAS A STAPLE OF PINEWOOD FALLS. ITS
checkered floors and wood-paneled walls radiated a warm, worn-in
charm. Locals filled the booths, laughing between bites of food, sharing
stories as the lunchtime bustle moved around them. The scent of
sizzling butter from breakfast still hung in the air, blending with the
savory aromas of the lunch rush. It was a comforting place, one where
people didn't just eat—they lingered, connected, made memories. But
for Sawyer, the familiarity only sharpened the edges of his unease.

Slipping into a corner booth, the leather seat creaked beneath him.
The sensation was oddly grounding, even as his mind churned. He
picked up the laminated menu, scanning it without really seeing the
words. His eyes moved across the list of items, but his brain stayed
stuck elsewhere, re-playing in his head like an unwelcome echo: *"They
know. You're running out of time."*

Sawyer's attention drifted to the steady hum of conversation around
him, the voices blending into a low murmur. The clink of silverware
sounded distant, like background noise to the whirl of thoughts he
couldn't shut off. *Was it a mistake coming here?*

He let the menu drop to the table with a soft thud, his hands curling
around the edge of it. Across the room, a group of teenagers laughed

over milkshakes, their carefree chatter so loud it momentarily cut through his thoughts. *They don't know how easy they have it,* he thought bitterly, the weight of his own troubles pressing harder.

His finger tapped absently on the edge of the table, wondering if anyone could tell how restless he felt beneath the calm facade.

Get a grip, he told himself. But it was easier said than done.

A waitress appeared beside him, her kind eyes offset by the no-nonsense demeanor of someone used to managing the midday crowd.

"Visiting or new in town?" she asked, pencil hovering over her notepad.

"Guess I stick out, huh?"

She chuckled, glancing around the room. "You're not one of the regulars. Here for the rally?"

Sawyer hesitated. "Sort of. I work for the senator."

The waitress leaned in, lowering her voice. The faint scent of spearmint and cigarettes followed her breath. "If I were you, I'd keep that under wraps. Folks around here aren't too thrilled about Masterson, not with what's happening to our water."

The weight of her words settled in the bottom of his stomach. "Thanks for the warning."

Her pencil moved to the notepad. "What can I get you?"

He glanced at the menu, barely registering the options. "Any recommendations?"

"Well, today's special is our house-made pot roast sandwich with hand-cut fries and a pickle spear. Or if you want something lighter, our Cranberry Turkey Salad's a local favorite—comes with dried cranberries, candied pecans, and maple balsamic dressing. And," she added with a grin, "you can't leave without trying our apple cider doughnuts. Baked fresh every morning."

"Make it the pot roast sandwich. And yeah, maybe an apple cider doughnut to go."

"Good choice," she said, scribbling down the order. "Coffee?"

"Sure, thanks."

As the waitress moved off, Sawyer leaned back in his seat. Framed photographs lined the walls. Mount Washington in every season—

snow-covered peaks, blazing autumn colors, and lush summer greenery. The windows revealed a view of the mountains in the distance, reminding him just how remote Pinewood Falls was.

The waitress returned a moment later, setting a steaming cup of coffee in front of him. "Food'll be up in no time."

Sawyer managed a smile until she turned away. His eyes flicked toward the door, nerves setting in as he stirred the coffee. Then he saw her.

A woman in a worn leather jacket slipped inside, the wind gusting behind her. Her eyes swept the room, alert, scanning until they locked on him. She moved quickly, sliding into the seat across from him, hands trembling as she reached for the coffee.

"Do you mind?" she asked, her voice tight.

"Looks like you need it more than me," Sawyer said, sliding the cup toward her.

"Thanks." She added sugar and took a long sip, the warmth seeming to calm her frayed edges. "Cold for spring. Don't remember it being this bad."

"Things are a changin'," he replied.

"I can't believe you just used one of Masterson's slogans on me."

"Who do you think came up with it?" He gave a playful bow of his head, tipping an imaginary hat with the showmanship of a ringmaster.

If things were different—if the world wasn't closing in on them—he might've asked her out. But even now, windswept and anxious, she was out of his league.

The waitress returned, setting his plate in front of him. "Didn't mention you had company coming," she teased. "Want to get anything for her?"

She shook her head. "I'll just steal some of his."

The waitress grinned. "Suit yourself. If you're still hungry after she eats all your food, let me know."

Sawyer waited until the waitress was out of earshot. He leaned forward, lowering his voice. "Glad you made it."

"I couldn't pass up the invitation," she said with forced levity, though the tension in her eyes betrayed her.

Sawyer exhaled slowly, pulling a small thumb drive from his pocket. Sliding it across the table, his hand lingered as if reluctant to let it go. "Everything you need is on there—documents, recordings, even some of Masterson's private emails. It's all laid out. Crystal Springs, the water deal—it's bigger than we thought."

"Before all this, I didn't understand how companies like Crystal Springs operated. Sure, I knew they were about profit. But this?" She shook her head. "They're predators, Sawyer. And we've all been blind to it."

Sawyer leaned forward, his voice dropping to a near whisper. "Most people don't want to see it. That's how companies like this survive. They buy the water rights, lock entire towns into ironclad contracts, and start bottling. By the time the locals figure out what's happening, it's too late. The wells are dry, the streams are poisoned, and they're stuck buying back their own water—at a premium."

Her brows furrowed. "And they sell it like it's some kind of gift. 'Bringing jobs back to America.' What a joke."

"Exactly." His gaze swept the other patrons, his jaw tightening. "What they don't advertise is the fallout. The environmental destruction from their plants, the small towns they bankrupt, or the families left with nothing but undrinkable water. They peddle the lie that they're saving the community, but they're robbing us blind and erasing the future at the same time."

Picking up the drive, her fingers tightened around it. "That's why we have to do this. Expose them. Wake people up to the truth."

"Once this gets out, we're targets," Sawyer said, his voice grim. "They'll come after us, and they won't stop."

Her eyes locked on his. "Let them come. If we don't do this, who will?"

Sawyer's expression hardened. "You're right. I can't stand by anymore. Masterson's in deep, and the people of Pinewood Falls deserve the truth."

"You're putting yourself out there, more than I am." She stared at the thumb drive, then took a deep breath. "They'll know it's you."

"I've been backing the wrong horse for too long," he admitted, lowering his voice. "I thought I could change things from the inside, but I've seen too much. I can't just sit on the sidelines anymore."

"Brave of you, standing up to them. Not many would."

He shook his head. "It's not bravery. It's survival."

For a moment, they sat in silence, sharing the food as the reality of what they were about to do settled over them.

She slipped the thumb drive into her jacket. "They won't know what hit them."

"Just promise me you'll be careful."

"I will," she replied, though they both knew caution might not be enough.

Sawyer slid a small manila envelope across the table. "Here—backup. In case anything happens to me."

She tucked it into her jacket. "Nothing's going to happen to you."

"I hope you're right," he said quietly. "But we both know the risks."

They shared a final, solemn glance. She stood, pulling her jacket tighter around her as she headed for the door, pushing through and out into the cold.

Sawyer was once again alone with his thoughts. He watched her go, a knot of dread tightening in his gut. Once the truth came out, there would be no going back. No running.

And no guarantee they'd make it out alive.

SEVEN

THE RAINSTORM HAD PASSED, LEAVING THE NIGHT AIR CRISP AND CLEAN. Fading storm clouds lingered on the horizon, streaked with moonlight, as the private jet descended toward a small airstrip outside Pinewood Falls. Hatch watched from her window, the wheels hissing against the slick tarmac as the jet touched down. The damp air carried the scent of pine and wet earth, a contrast to the metallic hum of the engines winding down.

As the plane taxied to a stop near a weathered hangar, Hatch felt the familiar twinge of anticipation, sharpened by a subtle edge of unease. Something about this quiet, isolated town nestled in the mountains made the stakes feel more immediate. Her fingers grazed the scar on her right arm, a habit she'd developed since Afghanistan, tracing the pattern of twisted skin—a permanent reminder that missions can go south in the blink of an eye.

At the edge of the tarmac, an SUV sat in the dim light, headlights off, silhouetted by the receding storm. A tall figure stepped out, his posture straight. As he approached, Hatch noticed the way he moved—calculated, eyes scanning the periphery as if he could sense trouble lurking in the shadows. Ethan Reeves, the man assigned to escort her, gave her a brief nod of acknowledgment.

"Ms. Hatch?" he asked, his voice sharp and professional, with a touch of wariness.

"That's me," she replied, shaking his hand firmly. "You must be Reeves."

"Ethan Reeves," he confirmed, his handshake equally firm but not lingering. "Head of security for Senator Masterson. I'll be driving you into town."

There was no animosity in his tone, but Hatch could read the tension—this was a man who didn't like surprises, and her presence was clearly one of them. She followed him to the SUV, the gravel crunching beneath their boots, the scent of fresh rain heavy in the cool air.

They drove in silence for the first few minutes, the engine's low hum filling the void between them. Hatch's eyes scanned the dark, wet roads outside, the small-town charm of Pinewood Falls revealing itself slowly as they drove past. Her eyes flicked to a freshly painted welcome sign on the town's outskirts, the bright colors clashing against the weathered wood beneath it. Quaint houses, wooden store-fronts, and sparse streetlights lined the main road. The scene stirred faint memories of Hawk's Landing, the quiet town she once called home.

But nostalgia wasn't why she was here.

Reeves finally broke the silence, his tone tight and guarded. "I'm not sure why the Senator felt the need to bring in someone from outside. My team's more than capable."

Hatch let the tension roll off her. "I don't doubt that. I'm here as an extra set of eyes, nothing more. Sometimes an outsider sees things others might miss."

"Support," Reeves replied, his skepticism barely hidden. "And what exactly are we looking for?"

Hatch let the question hang for a moment. "That's what we're here to find out, isn't it?"

As they neared the town center, the moonlight glinted off the wet streets, giving the picturesque town a surreal quality. Hatch took in the scene—small, peaceful, the kind of place where dark secrets could hide beneath the surface. She'd seen it before.

Reeves glanced down at the scar on her arm, his eyes lingering for a second longer than necessary.

"What happened?" he asked, keeping his tone neutral.

Hatch didn't look at him, her eyes still focused on the darkened landscape. "Afghanistan. Suicide bomber. I was lucky."

A flicker of understanding stretched across Reeves' face. "I've been in the sandbox. Know how fast things can go to shit. Split decisions made in a fraction of a second can alter the trajectory of the rest of your life."

"Yeah," Hatch said, her voice distant. "It happens like that sometimes. One minute you're on a routine patrol, the next..."

She trailed off, and Reeves didn't push. "True," he agreed quietly. There was a shift in his tone now, a softening, although he didn't drop his guard entirely.

"How long did you serve?" Hatch asked.

"Long enough to know when my luck was running out." Reeves cracked his knuckles. "Plus, who could pass up an easier life for better pay?"

She gestured to a scar snaking down his face to his jawline. "Is that the battle scar that gave you the epiphany?"

He nodded. "Everyone reaches their limit. Some aren't smart enough to realize it."

They drove on, the tension between them still present but no longer hostile. It was obvious he wasn't thrilled with her being here, but she didn't need his approval, nor was she seeking it.

They pulled up to a modest roadside motel, the neon sign flickering weakly against the night sky. Something familiar, comforting, in the simplicity of the motel.

"The Senator's staying at a house he's rented for the time he's here. Nice spot. Plenty of room. The other members of the team are there as well. You sure you don't want to switch accommodations? It'd be easier to keep everyone in the same place."

Hatch shook her head. "I'm more comfortable in places like this. Easier to spot anything out of place."

Reeves raised an eyebrow. "Suit yourself. The venue's about a mile up the mountain from here. I'll pick you up at 0700 to go over the op plan."

Hatch stepped out of the SUV, slinging her bag over her shoulder. She paused before closing the door. "I know you're not thrilled about this setup, but we're in this together. Something tells me we'll need to work as a team on this one."

Reeves hesitated for a moment before giving her a curt nod. "See you in the morning, Hatch."

As the SUV pulled away, Hatch stood alone in the dimly lit parking lot. She glanced up at the sky—the clouds had finally cleared, allowing the moon to peek through. The air smelled of pine and wet leaves, fresh and clean, but Hatch knew better.

She took a deep breath, then made her way to the motel lobby to check in. She went straight to her room after getting the key, dropped her bag on the bed and headed out the door.

THE RAINSTORM HAD CLEARED, leaving the night air crisp, with lingering mist clinging to the ground like ghostly fingers. Hatch zipped her jacket as she set off from her motel, the cool breeze carrying pine and damp earth. The climb to Evergreen Summit Lodge—the town's most prestigious resort—was steady, the narrow streets winding upward toward the hotel nestled in the foothills. Her boots crunched over the wet gravel, the sound unnervingly loud in the stillness. Her trained eye picked out potential hiding spots along the rocky outcroppings that bordered the town. In the distance, the faint glow of white-capped mountains under moonlight was beautiful yet ominous. The terrain was perfect for a sniper, and the thought sent a chill down her spine that had nothing to do with the evening air.

By the time she reached the lodge, Hatch's muscles were warmed, but her senses were still on edge. The resort loomed on high ground, its grand architecture bathed in the soft light of elegant lampposts. Rustic wooden beams and a stone facade gave it an air of luxury meant to blend into its natural surroundings. But to Hatch, it stood out like a beacon—a target.

The moment she entered the lobby, she was assaulted by a mix of sounds and smells. The rich aroma of roasted meats and fine spirits drifted from the dining room to her right, where glasses clinked, and low conversation mingled with soft music. To her left, a frustrated guest's voice rose above the general din at the check-in desk.

"This is unacceptable!" the woman snapped at the frazzled desk clerk. "I specifically requested a mountain-view suite!"

Hatch tuned out the complaint as she continued her visual sweep of the room. A brick fireplace flickered warmly in the center, casting a golden glow over a family of four playing Monopoly at a low table surrounded by leather couches. The idyllic setting clashed with the knot of tension forming in her gut.

Ahead, a carved wooden sign pointed toward the hallway leading to the banquet hall and guest rooms. Hatch's attention shifted to a nearby chess table, where a man sat half-shrouded in shadow, wearing a heavy coat and a ballcap pulled low over his face. His hands absently toyed with a bishop piece, but what stood out was how his eyes scanned the room without moving his head—a telltale sign of someone assessing their surroundings.

Her instincts prickled, the familiar sensation tightening in her chest. She kept her pace casual, passing him without making direct eye contact, but her senses remained tuned to his every movement. His rugged appearance, combined with the intensity in his posture, sent warning signals. Something about him didn't sit right, but Hatch moved on, heading toward the hallway.

She pulled open the banquet hall doors and stepped inside. The faint smell of fresh paint and cleaning products lingered in the air, mingling with the soft clatter of chairs being arranged by hotel employees. Rows of seats were being positioned in neat lines, each one narrowing the walking space, creating potential hazards for evacuation. Hatch's gaze flicked to the expansive windows at the far end of the room. The view of the mountain vista was stunning—peaks still capped in the remnants of winter snow—but it made her stomach tighten.

Beautiful, but dangerous. The windows were a security nightmare, offering unobstructed sightlines for anyone outside with a scoped rifle. Her mind automatically calculated the distances, considering angles and potential cover spots. *If someone's out there, we'd never see them until it's too late.*

She moved slowly through the space, her eyes cataloging every detail. The two primary exits were wide and easily accessible, but that also made them vulnerable to an ambush. The smaller door in the back corner was narrow and partially obscured by a folding partition—*an easy bottleneck if panic sets in.* The catering entrance off to the side had a swinging door, its porthole window offering just enough visibility to spot movement from the kitchen.

The rows of chairs were tightly packed, creating choke points that could funnel people into confined spaces during an emergency. *This many bodies in one place—it's a recipe for chaos if anything goes sideways.* Her gaze drifted upward to the recessed lighting and ceiling panels. No visible cameras or rigging for surveillance—*a blind spot that's begging to be exploited.*

Hatch paused by the podium at the front of the room, running a hand along the edge of the wood. From here, the senator would be completely exposed. The raised platform gave him visibility to the crowd, but it also left him vulnerable from nearly every angle. She turned, scanning the audience area again. *We'll need at least one person near the stage and another near the back wall. Eyes everywhere. And someone needs to secure the kitchen access—it's too close to the main event space.*

It was the kind of place where things could turn ugly fast if security wasn't airtight. And judging by the setup so far, Hatch knew there was work to be done.

"Excuse me, ma'am?" a young employee with a clipboard approached. "Are you with the event staff?"

Hatch nodded. "Just getting a lay of the land. Big day tomorrow, right?"

"Yes, ma'am. Biggest event we've had all year."

She slipped out through the doors on the opposite side of the fireplace, re-entering the lobby. Her eyes flicked back to the chess table. The man was gone.

Alarm bells rang in her head as she spotted him moving toward the far hallway, his shoulders hunched, head down. He dipped his head low, using the brim of the hat to obscure his face as if deliberately avoiding the security camera in the corner. His movements were quick, purposeful.

Hatch's pulse quickened, adrenaline spiking as she followed. Just as she neared the side exit, a group of rowdy teens barreled down the stairs, laughing and shoving, towels slung over their shoulders. They crashed into Hatch, nearly knocking her off balance.

"Watch it!" she snapped, frustration lacing her voice as she steadied herself.

"Sorry, lady!" one of the teens called back, barely bothering to sound apologetic.

By the time Hatch cleared the teenagers, the man was gone. She cursed under her breath, pushing through the side exit and stepping into the cool night. Her breath hung in the air as she scanned the parking lot. An engine revved nearby, drawing her attention just as blinding headlights flashed on. A Jeep sat idling, its lights aimed directly at her, obscuring the driver.

Squinting through the glare, Hatch shielded her eyes, trying to make out the silhouette behind the wheel. The man lingered just long enough to make sure she saw him before peeling out, tires kicking up gravel as the Jeep roared away into the night.

Hatch stood still for a beat, her senses still heightened, adrenaline coursing through her veins. Something wasn't right. Whoever that man was, he wasn't just a passerby.

As the taillights of the Jeep disappeared down the road, Hatch exhaled slowly, her breath visible in the cold night air. She'd need to bring this up with Reeves first thing in the morning. But for now, she had time to think—and prepare for whatever lay ahead.

EIGHT

THE COOL MORNING AIR BIT AT RACHEL HATCH'S FACE AS SHE STEPPED outside her motel room, her boots crunching softly on the gravel. A black SUV idled by the curb, its engine humming in the quiet dawn. The streets of Pinewood Falls were just beginning to stir, the scent of fresh-baked bread from the nearby bakery mingling with the crisp mountain air. Hatch had already completed her morning run, cataloging the town's potential vulnerabilities—the narrow alleyways, the overgrown mining tunnels snaking through the hillside, and the dilapidated structures perfect for hiding. But her mind kept circling back to the man she'd seen the night before. The man who didn't belong.

Reeves stood by the SUV, arms crossed, his expression impenetrable. The man was efficient, no-nonsense, and he still clearly wasn't thrilled about Hatch's involvement. She kept her own body language neutral. Friction between them wasn't going to help the mission.

"Morning," Hatch greeted, shaking off the last traces of chill from her skin.

"Figured I'd pick you up early. We've got a walkthrough in an hour, but I want to go over a few things first." He pulled open the passenger door—a motion that felt more like formality than courtesy.

Sliding into the seat, Hatch felt the low rumble of the engine beneath her. As the SUV pulled away, she glanced out the window. Quaint shops with hand-painted signs, old-fashioned lampposts, and hanging baskets of mountain flowers blurred by.

"I saw something last night," Hatch started, keeping her voice deliberately casual. "A guy in the lobby at the resort—muddy boots, baseball cap pulled low, and he was avoiding the cameras like it was second nature. You got anyone from your team posted there?"

Reeves didn't take his eyes off the road. "Nobody from my team was on-site. This town draws all kinds. Could be nothing. Could just be some drifter."

The dismissiveness in his tone grated on Hatch, but she held back, instead casting her eyes toward the looming Evergreen Summit Lodge, its elegant exterior gleaming in the early light. To a casual observer, it was a luxury resort nestled into the rugged mountains. To Hatch, it looked more like a bullseye.

They soon arrived at the senator's rented estate—an imposing, high-end home nestled in the foothills. The security team was already in place, and the tension in the air was thick enough to cut. Reeves parked, and Hatch adjusted her jacket, her hand briefly brushing the Glock hidden beneath it—a comforting presence.

Inside the home, Hatch was introduced to Senator William Masterson. Reeves' voice was tight as he garnered Masterson's attention. "Senator, this is Rachel Hatch. She's here to add extra protection to your detail, per your request."

He had the practiced confidence of a career politician—sharp eyes that appraised her in a heartbeat, a firm handshake that spoke of control, and an air of authority that demanded attention. His aide, Nathan Sawyer, hovered nearby, clearly uncomfortable in the presence of so many hardened professionals. He seemed as out of place as a lamb in a den of wolves.

Masterson's calculating eyes lingered on Hatch for a moment. "Ms. Hatch, I appreciate your presence. With any luck, your services will only be necessary for this morning's town hall meeting we're holding at the resort."

Hatch returned the look, as if eyeing the man back could tell her everything she needed to know about him. The devil was always in the details. But this wasn't her op, she reminded herself. She was just an extra body. Nothing more. "Just here to make sure everything runs smoothly, Senator."

Masterson's tone shifted, revealing a flicker of unease behind his polished exterior. "The threats we've received have been unsettling, to say the least. But nothing concrete so far, right?" He glanced at Reeves, seeking reassurance.

"Not really," Reeves said, his voice calm but firm. "Most of the threats are vague—anonymous letters and emails. The usual noise. "

Hatch's brow furrowed. "Anything specific in the threats? "

"Like I said, it's just noise for now. Everyone's got an opinion these days. With all the social media platforms, every asshole with a keyboard can wage their own personal war. Lucky for us, they rarely act on it." Reeves' tone was almost dismissive. "Don't get me wrong. That doesn't mean we can afford to let our guard down. It only takes one lunatic to turn words into action."

Reeves motioned for the team to gather around the large table in the conference room, where maps and logistics sheets were spread out in meticulous order. He quickly took charge of the briefing, his delivery rehearsed and methodical.

"Arrival is set for 11:00," he began, tracing the route on the map with his finger. "We'll be moving in a three-car caravan. The senator and Nathan will be in the middle car. We'll be entering through the main lobby. That's our tightest spot, the most vulnerable. Local law enforcement will be managing protestors outside, and once we get the senator inside, it's a straight shot to the banquet hall."

Hatch's eyes followed the route on the map, memorizing every detail as Reeves continued outlining the plan. Reeves discussed potential choke points, escape routes, and places where an attacker could strike. He'd hit on most of the weaknesses her previous night's reconnaissance had gathered.

"Once the senator is onstage and security is in place, we'll let citizens in for the meeting. Protestors will remain outside. Afterward, we'll escort the senator through the side exit to the vehicles, and we're out. Any questions?"

Hatch's attention lingered on the high ground she'd scouted the night before, the memory of that man—avoiding the cameras—nagging at her.

"That elevated terrain outside the resort could pose a problem," she said, pointing to the map. "It's wide open. Perfect vantage point."

Reeves frowned, a flash of irritation crossing his face. "We'll have it covered. But so far, there's no indication of any serious threat."

"Any serious, well-planned threat isn't going to reveal itself until it's already too late." Hatch pressed. "That man I mentioned.. He didn't strike me as a tourist."

"I'll pass the description on to the sheriff. He and his deputies will be our eyes on the ground before we arrive."

Hatch could infer from his tone, his message clear. This discussion was over.

"Sounds like I'm in good hands." Masterson glanced between them. " Let's stay sharp."

The room fell into a heavy silence, the tension between Hatch and Reeves palpable. Reeves wasn't entirely sold on her input, but she wasn't here to win a popularity contest. Her job was to make sure the senator got through this event alive, and she wasn't about to let a dismissive attitude get in the way.

As the briefing wrapped up, Hatch couldn't shake the feeling that the man at the lodge was no drifter. Her instincts—those she had learned to trust over years in the field—told her they were grossly underprepared for whatever was coming.

And if she was right, they wouldn't see it until it was too late.

NINE

TWELVE HOURS. HE HAD BEEN IN POSITION FOR TWELVE LONG HOURS, HIS body pressed into the cold, damp ground. Patience was a virtue in his line of work, one honed through years of grueling missions and endless waits. Each shift in his muscles was deliberate, every breath measured. Inhaling slowly, he could still smell the faint remnants of last night's rain, mingling with the earthy scent of moss and pine needles. A bead of sweat trickled down his temple, despite the chill—a reminder of the tension coiled within him.

The wind whispered over the rocky outcropping, its cold fingers tugging at his camouflaged ghillie suit. He lay flat against the jagged rock, his body melded with the terrain, a still shadow amidst the wild backdrop of the White Mountains. The vantage point he had chosen was perfect—a sniper's paradise. From this elevated position, he had a clear, unobstructed line of sight to the side entrance of the hotel below, the same exit he had slipped through the previous night.

Reaching into the pocket of his vest, his fingers brushed over the comforting bag of fireball candies—his only vice. He unwrapped one and tucked it between his teeth, savoring the burn as the cinnamon hit his tongue. It kept him sharp, grounded. The familiar taste transported him, if only for a moment, to a dusty Afghan mountaintop where the habit had begun. The memory flickered and faded, replaced by the cold reality of the mission ahead.

The rifle—a custom bolt-action, chambered for .338 Lapua Magnum —lay nestled beside him, dialed in perfectly. He had spent hours adjusting the scope, compensating for the wind, humidity, and altitude. The bipod was locked into place, the barrel a steady extension of himself, aimed directly at the hotel's side entrance. Precision was his language, and in this language, there were no second chances.

His setup was meticulous, every piece of gear camouflaged to blend seamlessly with the season's foliage. A small rodent scurried past, inches from his face, oblivious to his presence. He wasn't there. Not to them.

Through the scope, he tracked the hotel with surgical precision. The crosshairs hovered over the side door—the one Senator William Masterson would use after the town hall meeting. The senator's security team had swept the area, but they hadn't found him. They wouldn't. This was his domain. He had been left for dead once and survived— crossing nearly a hundred miles of enemy territory with nothing but a broken radio and a knife. Waiting here for the perfect shot was child's play.

His thoughts drifted to the woman from the lobby. The scar on her arm. Her posture. She had the look of someone who had been there— someone who had danced close to death and survived. An operator. But she wasn't his target.

Masterson had sold out other towns like Pinewood Falls, trading their lifeblood for corporate favors. This wasn't just a hit—it was justice. Still, in the back of his mind, a whisper asked: is this justice, or vengeance? He shoved the doubt aside.

The distant chants of protesters reached his ears. Sweeping his scope over them briefly, He caught the signs they held aloft. "Our Water, Our Rights," one read. His gaze lingered for just a moment longer than necessary. His focus muted the noise. They were irrelevant to his mission.

Then, movement. The convoy.

Three black SUVs snaked up the winding road toward the hotel, their polished exteriors glinting in the afternoon sun. The protestors surged, but law enforcement held them at bay as the vehicles came to a stop. Security swarmed, and the tension in the air thickened.

His finger rested lightly on the trigger. The world beyond his scope didn't matter. The only thing was the target and the crosshairs oscillating over his chest.

.

TEN

EVELYN HARTWELL'S FINGERS GRIPPED THE STEERING WHEEL TIGHTLY, HER knuckles white against the cracked leather, as the swell of protesters surged in front of her. The voices of the crowd, loud and angry, echoed off the nearby buildings, homemade signs bobbed in the air like banners of defiance. Pinewood Falls had never seen anything like this. Chloe sat beside her, practically vibrating with excitement, clutching the colorful protest flyer in her hands like it was a sacred artifact. Despite the knot of anxiety twisting in her stomach, Evelyn couldn't help but warm at her daughter's boundless enthusiasm.

"I still don't know why you insisted we come," Evelyn said, the edge in her voice softening as she glanced at Chloe. The girl had always had a way of convincing Evelyn to do things she'd normally avoid, just like her father used to.

"Because it's important," Chloe replied, her hazel eyes flashing with the same fierce determination that Evelyn had once admired in her husband. "They can't just take our water and expect us to sit back. If we don't fight, we lose."

Evelyn sighed, her grip tightening until the leather creaked under her fingers. "I know, sweetie. I just don't want you getting mixed up in this. It's going to get loud, and people might start getting upset."

"Good," Chloe shot back, her voice sharpening. "They should be upset. Look what they did to Mr. Johnson's farm!"

The image of Tom Johnson's withered crops flashed through Evelyn's mind, the dry earth of his once-fertile fields cracked and barren. Chloe was right—Masterson's deal with Crystal Springs had bled the town dry, just like the water they siphoned off. Still, protesting wasn't in Evelyn's nature. She was the type to hope things would work out if she kept her head down. But maybe that wasn't enough anymore.

They pulled into a parking spot, the crunch of gravel beneath the tires barely audible over the growing noise of the rally. The air was thick with the mingling scents of sweat, dirt, and pine. Evelyn spotted Liam near the front of the protest, waving a sign that read *Save Our Town! Keep Our Water!* His tall frame towered over the crowd, and when he saw them, his face lit up with an energy that was hard to come by in these days of drought and despair.

"Ms. Hartwell! Chloe!" He was breathless but smiling as he jogged toward them. "I'm glad you made it!"

Chloe bolted from the car before Evelyn had a chance to unbuckle her seatbelt. "I told you we'd come!"

Evelyn climbed out more cautiously, scanning the faces in the crowd. The turnout was larger than she'd expected—impressive, yes, but unnerving. The air felt charged, like the moment before a thunderstorm, full of restless energy ready to explode. A prickle of unease crawled up her spine.

"This is quite the crowd," she said to Liam as she stepped closer. His sign still gleamed with fresh paint, and Evelyn could almost feel the determination radiating from him.

Liam glanced over his shoulder. "Yeah, Dad's near the entrance trying to keep things under control. He's … worried it might get ugly."

Evelyn looked over to Sheriff Tuck, his broad frame cutting a path through the sea of protesters. The sun glinted off his badge, a reminder of the authority he wielded. He looked as steady as ever, but the subtle tension in his shoulders hinted that he sensed the fragile balance that could snap at any moment.

"Maybe I should go say hi," Evelyn murmured, though the flutter in her chest betrayed the casualness of her words.

Liam grinned at the suggestion. "He'd like that. He's been stressed. More than usual, I mean."

Chloe tugged at her mother's sleeve, her voice bubbling with excitement. "Can I go with Liam, Mom? Please? I want to get closer to the front!"

Evelyn hesitated, looking over at the gathering crowd. The rally was peaceful *for now*, but the undercurrent of tension was undeniable. "Just stay close, okay? If anything feels wrong, come right back."

"I promise," Chloe said, already tugging Liam toward the thick of the protest. "We'll be careful!"

Evelyn watched them disappear into the crowd, pride and fear mingling in her chest. Chloe had her father's determination—a trait Evelyn admired but couldn't control. She just hoped that fiery spirit wouldn't get her daughter into trouble.

Taking a breath, she made her way toward the sheriff. The crowd parted slightly. He noticed her approach, a faint, familiar smile touching his lips. For a moment, Evelyn felt a warmth she hadn't felt in a long time.

"Evelyn," he greeted, his voice low but welcoming. "Didn't expect to see you here. Everything okay?"

She glanced down as she spoke. "I wasn't planning on it, but Chloe insisted. She's as stubborn as ever."

A low chuckle escaped him. "Yeah, she gets that from you. Always pushing, always fighting for what's right."

Evelyn raised an eyebrow. "Well, Liam's surely becoming quite the spirited young man."

"Don't know where he gets it from." He shrugged.

For a moment, the noise of the protest faded, and they stood there, sharing a rare moment of peace. But then his expression hardened, his eyes scanning the crowd once more.

"I've got to keep an eye on things," he said, his voice growing tense. "More people showed up than I expected. Some troublemakers from out of town, too. Trying to keep this thing from getting out of hand is a tall order for me and my deputies. We're stretched thin as it is."

Evelyn's unease deepened. The chants were growing louder, angrier. The tension she'd felt earlier was no longer just a passing thought—it was real, thick enough to taste in the air.

"I should get back to Chloe," she said, but she lingered, the weight of his presence comforting in a way she hadn't expected. "Just...be careful, okay?"

"I will," he promised, his tone softening. He dropped his authoritative sheriff's role, exchanging it for a more casual one. "You take care of yourself, too. Liam told me that Covington guy was giving you a hard time the other day. I'll have a talk with him."

"No need to get involved. He's wasting his time if he thinks he's gonna get me to move. Heard he got Malcom Trent to sign. Guess that makes me the last holdout."

A roar from the crowd startled her.

Tuck's response was muffled by the ruckus. He leaned in close. His breath brushed against her ear as he spoke. "Gotta go. But I'll stop by later."

As Evelyn turned back to the crowd, the sound of sirens sliced through the chanting, signaling the senator's arrival. Almost immediately, the crowd surged forward, pressing against the barricades, their voices rising to a fever pitch.

No water, no peace! No water, no peace!

The chant was deafening now, the anger palpable. Evelyn's pulse quickened as she spotted the sleek black SUVs pulling up to the entrance. The energy in the air had shifted, anticipation giving way to something more dangerous. She felt the press of bodies around her, the heat of frustration, the ragged breath of people who had been pushed too far.

She found Chloe and Liam near the front, their signs held high, their voices joining the chorus of fury. Evelyn's heart swelled with pride, but also dread. She pulled Chloe closer, gripping her wrist tightly.

"Stay by me," Evelyn told her daughter, her eyes darting around the crowd. "We might need to leave soon."

"But Mom we're making a difference! You can feel it, can't you?"

Before Evelyn could respond, the SUVs came to a stop. The senator stepped out and climbed onto the running board, positioning himself above the crowd. His arms outstretched like the wings of a hawk, poised to swoop down on unsuspecting prey. The chants grew louder, swelling into a deafening roar that reverberated through the air.

Evelyn pushed back through the crowd, her focus locked on Chloe. She swam upstream in the surge of protestors, her shoulders brushing against signs and flailing arms. The press of bodies was suffocating, each step forward a struggle against the tide. The air grew thick with heat and tension, the smell of sweat and frustration clinging to her like a second skin.

Around her, the crowd began to surge, a chaotic ripple as protestors collided with the deputies. Shouts turned to screams as the deputies strained to contain the mass of people, their line buckling like a dam on the verge of collapse. A protestor stumbled and fell, tripping those behind him and triggering a domino effect that sent bodies toppling.

"Chloe!" Evelyn shouted, her voice barely cutting through the cacophony. She shoved her way toward the edge of the commotion, her pulse pounding as the chaos spiraled. Deputies shouted commands, their words lost in the clamor. Protestors scrambled to stay upright, their signs waving wildly above the fray.

The deputies were a dam on the verge of collapse.

ELEVEN

Hatch's muscles coiled beneath her jacket as she scanned the hotel's banquet hall. The air hung heavy with the mingled scents of coffee, sweat, and barely concealed tension. Senator Masterson's voice boomed from the stage, but Hatch's focus flickered from face to face in the crowd, cataloging every furrowed brow and restless shift.

"Smalltown New Hampshire is the backbone of this state," Masterson declared, his words echoing off the walls. Yet beneath the senator's practiced confidence, Hatch sensed the crowd's simmering unease. Low murmurs, sharp and biting, slithered beneath the senator's speech, growing louder with each passing second.

Reeves stood near the stage, his jaw clenched, eyes fixed on Masterson. Behind the podium, Nathan Sawyer sat with his hands folded, his neutral expression betraying a flicker of concern as the undercurrent in the room grew darker.

In Hatch's earpiece, the comm crackled. "Eyes sharp," came the low, steady voice of one of her team. "Intel suggests potential agitators in the crowd."

The first person at the microphone was a supporter, but his praise for the senator barely made a dent in the charged atmosphere. Hatch's eyes swept across the room again. She spotted a woman moving with purpose toward the mic, her shoulders squared. Something about her stride—a determined, cutting edge—set Hatch's nerves on alert.

Here's an improved version of the dialogue, focusing on building tension and emphasizing the facts with sharper delivery and stronger pacing:

THE WOMAN GRIPPED the microphone tightly, her knuckles white, her voice cutting through the thin applause like a blade. "Isn't it true, Senator, that you're in bed with Crystal Springs?"

The room froze. Conversations died mid-sentence, and Hatch could almost hear the collective gasp ripple through the crowd. All eyes locked on the stage, the weight of the question hanging in the air like a storm cloud about to burst.

Masterson's practiced smile faltered, the polished veneer cracking just enough to reveal a flicker of unease. "I'm sorry, could you repeat your name?" he asked, his tone a thin attempt at control.

"Answer the question," the woman shot back, her voice sharp and unrelenting. "They're your biggest campaign contributor, aren't they? And isn't it true you sit on their board? Silent, of course. Profiting while our town's water is drained, bottled, and sold back to us at triple the price."

A murmur rippled through the crowd, low and angry, like the growl of a gathering storm. Hatch's pulse quickened as her eyes darted across the room. The tension was palpable, ready to ignite with a single spark.

The dam broke. The crowd's silence shattered as shouts erupted from all corners of the room, rolling toward the stage like an avalanche. "Sellout!" "Thief!" Anger, hot and acrid, filled the air.

"Now, let's all calm down—" Masterson began, but his words were swallowed by the rising tide of fury.

Hatch's heart raced, her senses going razor-sharp. She met Reeves' eyes across the room, his expression taut. He was already moving, speaking fast into his comm.

Reeves' voice crackled in her earpiece. "It's turning ugly. We're pulling him out. Prepare for extraction."

Chairs scraped against the floor as people stood, their agitation spreading like wildfire. Hatch moved fluidly, cutting through the chaos as she positioned herself by the exit. Her hand hovered near her concealed weapon but drawing it would be a last resort.

The crowd surged, their anger growing louder, more desperate. A plastic water bottle sailed through the air, narrowly missing Masterson. Hatch's body tensed, ready to act, but Reeves was already guiding the senator offstage, keeping his body between Masterson and the crowd.

The roar of the crowd followed them, a wave of noise pressing closer. Hatch's hand clenched the door handle, her eyes scanning the sea of faces one last time. Fear, anger, desperation—bitter emotions were written in the people's eyes, but beneath it all, a line had been crossed.

She yanked the door open, ushering Masterson and Reeves through. The heavy wood slammed shut behind them, cutting off the cacophony, but Hatch's gut told her this wasn't over.

The hallway was quiet. But just as she exhaled, the distant shouts grew louder. The protesters outside. Hatch's pulse spiked. They were pushing through, overwhelming the sheriff and his deputies.

"Reeves, we've got a breach," Hatch said into her comm, already moving, her body tense. The chaos from the banquet room was spilling into the hall, and the lobby wouldn't hold for long.

THE AIR CRACKLED with tension as protesters burst through the doors, their shouts echoing against the high ceilings. Gasps rippled through the hall, followed by the screech of chairs scraping against the floor as people stumbled back. Security stiffened, hands flying to their earpieces, unprepared for the situation that escalated so quickly.

Hatch's world sharpened, each detail gaining more clarity. The chaos around her became a blur as her focus narrowed. Bodies jostled in the crowd, the acrid scent of fear and sweat thick in the air.

Then she saw him—a hulking figure bulldozing through the throng. He was massive, his shoulders wide as a battering ram, eyes blazing with fury as they locked onto the senator. Hatch's pulse quickened as she started to move.

Reeves was focused on the senator, ushering him toward the exit. "We need to move, now," he barked into the comm, his voice hard with urgency, unaware of the storm brewing behind him.

"I've got this." Hatch's words cold and focused as she broke into a sprint.

The protester barreled forward, swinging a protest sign mounted on a heavy 2x4, his movements wild but disturbingly deliberate. He surged into the hallway from the main lobby, where the crowd was still pouring in, their voices swelling into a chaotic roar. People scattered in his wake, yelps of fear blending into the rising clamor.

The hallway connected the banquet hall to a side entrance, but now it felt like a trap, narrowing as the protester gained speed. The crowd instinctively parted, creating an unbroken path that led directly to the senator.

Hatch moved like water, cutting through the throng with practiced precision. Her steps were silent but swift, her focus locked on the threat. Every muscle in her body coiled, ready to spring. Her heartbeat thudded in her ears, keeping time with the protester's pounding footsteps. He was only seconds away from colliding with Masterson.

Not today.

Hatch's voice lashed out, sharp and commanding, freezing the man mid-stride. "Hey!"

He turned, eyes wild with rage, locking onto her. For a heartbeat, he hesitated, his eyes flicking over the woman before him. Underestimating her. His grip on the 2x4 tightened, and he swung with all his weight.

The wood whistled through the air, a brutal arc aimed at her.

But Hatch was faster. She slipped inside his guard, her body moving with fluid grace. The 2x4 skimmed past her shoulder, close enough that she felt the rush of air, but too slow to touch her.

Time slowed. She caught his arm, twisted, and used his momentum against him. Her body pivoted, muscles tensing as she sent his massive frame airborne. He flipped over her, a mess of limbs and fury.

The sound of his impact was deafening. He crashed onto a nearby table—the same one where the family had played Monopoly just the night before. Wood splintered beneath him, the table collapsing with a thunderous crack.

The protester groaned, his head lolling to the side, eyes glazed. He lay sprawled in the wreckage, his bulk shifting slightly as he teetered on the edge of unconsciousness. All the rage drained from his slackened face.

Hatch straightened, breathing in steady, measured bursts. The adrenaline surged through her system, but her focus was unshaken. She scanned the room, already assessing, calculating the next potential threat.

The hall had gone still, the chaos suspended in shocked silence. The other protesters stopped dead in their tracks after witnessing the big man toppled. Eyes fell on the woman who had dropped him with frightening ease. Their collective will faltered, uncertainty rippling through them.

Heavy boots thudded against the floor, and the sheriff rushed in, his face flushed with exertion. His eyes darted from the groaning protester to Hatch. Surprise flickered across his face, quickly replaced by a surprised respect.

The sheriff bent down, snapping handcuffs onto the man's wrists with a loud *click*. "Nice work," he muttered, his voice low, as though trying not to reveal just how impressed he was.

Hatch barely acknowledged the comment, her mind already moving ahead. The danger hadn't passed. She spotted Reeves ushering Masterson toward the side exit.

Hatch slipped behind Sawyer who was standing just behind the senator. The side door hissed shut behind them, cutting off the chaotic noise inside the hotel. Hatch's senses, still sharp from the earlier confrontation, scanned the perimeter. The late morning sun bore down, harsh and unforgiving, casting long shadows from the nearby trees. The crisp air carried the scent of pine, sweat, and tension, but it did little to cool the heat of the situation brewing around them.

For a heartbeat, silence reigned. Then, like an unstoppable wave, the protesters' chants swelled from outside of the building, growing louder and angrier with each passing second.

Reeves stood beside Senator Masterson, his broad frame taut with frustration as he snarled into his radio. "Where the hell is the motorcade? Get those vehicles moving! Find a way around the protesters, now!"

Sawyer lingered off to the right, pale and jittery. His eyes flicked between the road—where their escape should have been waiting—and the angry crowd pressing against the barricades. The senator stood in the middle of it all, outwardly composed but unable to mask the slight tremble in his hands. His eyes darted to Hatch, seeking some unspoken reassurance.

Hatch's instincts hummed, her mind analyzing. The line of trees at the property's edge offered too many places for someone to hide. The rocky outcroppings, the faulty security perimeter, the growing unrest. It all screamed danger. She shifted closer to the senator, her muscles coiled tight, ready to spring into action.

"Dammit, they're blocking the road," Reeves growled, his back turned for a moment as the garbled response crackled in his earpiece. When he spun back around, his eyes were blazing. His usual ironclad composure was slipping, each second stretching the tension taut. "I don't care how—find a way through!"

Hatch ran through the events leading up to this choke point. The delayed motorcade, the rising fury of the crowd, the lack of cover in their current position—it was a security disaster waiting to happen. Her eyes never stopped moving, tracking every shift in the environment, cataloging every possible threat.

Then she felt it. A prickling sensation down the back of her neck—the unmistakable sense of being watched.

Reeves was pacing now, barking into the radio, each word clipped with frustration. "Move them! I don't care how—clear the damn path!"

The senator stood like a statue, jaw clenched so tight Hatch could almost hear his teeth grinding. Sawyer's nervous energy manifested in a constant shuffle, his feet never staying still for long.

Hatch caught a glint in the distance—just a brief flicker of light reflecting off something metallic, hidden among the rocks. The realization hit her like a jolt of electricity. She tensed, her muscles primed for action.

And then it happened.

A sharp crack ripped through the air—a high-powered rifle shot, unmistakable and deadly. The sound split the through the protestors' shouts, echoing across the grounds.

TWELVE

THE CRACK OF THE RIFLE SHOT ECHOED OFF THE MOUNTAINSIDE, SHARP and final. For a moment, time froze. Then everything snapped back to life.

The protesters surged forward in a chaotic wave, their angry chants morphing into screams. Bodies collided, frantic and desperate, all of them crashing toward the senator. Masterson's security team sprang into action with military precision. Reeves was barking orders, his voice cutting through the confusion as the team formed a human shield around their principal.

Hatch's senses lit up, every nerve screaming. The shot hadn't come from the crowd. The clean echo off the rocks, the sharpness of the report—this was no handgun. This was a high-caliber rifle, fired from a distance.

Her eyes swept the jagged outcroppings that surrounded the hotel. *Sniper.* The word flashed in her mind like a warning beacon. *High ground, line of sight. They're smart, trained.* Her heart thudded in her chest, but her breathing stayed steady. *Think. Find them. Counter the angle.*

She scanned the ridgelines, her gaze moving systematically. *Cover. Concealment. Where would I be?* The rocks offered endless shadows and crevices, any of which could shield a shooter. The glass facade of the hotel was a liability, reflecting light in erratic patterns. *A mirror for them, a trap for us.*

Hatch dropped her gaze briefly to the crowd. They were panicked, scattering in unpredictable patterns—perfect for sowing chaos, but terrible for control. *If I were them, this is when I'd take the second shot. Amplify the fear. Lock us down.*

Her hand instinctively hovered near her sidearm. *No time to hesitate. Find the shooter or find the next cover. The principal is exposed, and whoever's behind that rifle isn't here to make a statement—they're here to kill.*

There, perched on the jagged outcropping above the hotel, shadows danced across uneven rock faces. Sparse patches of scrub and dried grass clung to the crags, offering minimal cover but enough for a skilled marksman. The sun glinted off something—a flash of metal. Gone in an instant, but unmistakable.

"Sniper!" Hatch's voice sliced through the din, sharp and urgent. "High ground, rocky overlook—ten o'clock from the main entrance! Partial cover, glint of metal—possibly scoped!" "Move!" Reeves roared, his hand already yanking Masterson toward the SUV. The security team tightened around the senator, bodies in motion, protective shields rising in practiced unison. The second shot never came, but the danger was a noose tightening around them.

Hatch's eyes darted back to the sniper's position, but it was empty. The shooter had already vanished, blending into the terrain. She snapped her attention to the crowd once more, but the protesters were oblivious, focused on the senator, their rage at full boil.

The SUV door swung open, and Reeves shoved Masterson inside. Relief flickered through Hatch—but a small, nagging detail wouldn't leave her alone. Something she hadn't seen yet.

Then she saw him.

Nathan Sawyer.

Slumped against the wall, his suit drenched in blood. The crimson soaked into the concrete beneath him, pooling in a dark, spreading stain. His face—usually composed, always professional—twisted with agony.

"Reeves!" Hatch's shout was raw, edged with urgency. "Sawyer's hit!"

Reeves glanced back, but he had no time to act. The senator was the mission. The motorcade roared to life, tires screeching as it peeled away, the rest of the security team following suit.

Hatch bolted to Sawyer's side, her knees hitting the ground hard. Blood pumped from his chest in rhythmic spurts—too much blood. Too fast. Her mind worked quickly, assessing.

Entry wound, upper left chest—likely through-and-through given the exit stain on the wall behind him. Arterial. His breathing's shallow—lungs compromised. Immediate priority: stop the bleed. Secondary: get him out of the kill zone.

She grabbed his suit and hauled him into the hallway, dragging him away from the exposed door.

She dropped beside him again, pressing her hands hard over the wound. Bright red liquid covered them instantly.

"Hold on, Sawyer. Hold on." The words came automatically, her focus entirely on staunching the bleeding. His chest heaved, each breath a shallow, painful rasp.

Sawyer's hand shot up, clutching at her sleeve, his grip weak but desperate. "Maggie....." The word gurgled out in a blood-choked whisper, his panic-stricken eyes locking onto hers, wide with fear and something else—regret? Pleading?

Hatch pressed harder, but the blood kept coming. His pulse fluttered beneath her hands, fading. His skin was pale, clammy, the color draining from his face. "Stay with me, Sawyer. I've got you."

But even as she said it, she knew the truth. The shot had torn through something vital. She could feel his life slipping away under her palms.

Sawyer's chest rose once more, a shallow, rattling breath, and then ... stillness.

Hatch stared down at him, the weight of his final word—*Maggie*—hung in the air, a question she couldn't answer. Slowly, she pulled her hands away from his body. Blood stained her fingers and palms, slick and warm. Her heart pounded in her chest, a sharp contrast to the stillness of the man beneath her.

Footsteps pounded down the hallway, the sheriff appearing at her side, breathless. "What the hell happened?"

THE SHERIFF DROPPED to his knees beside Nathan Sawyer's lifeless body, his face pale with shock, eyes wide with disbelief. Hatch could still feel the slick, sticky warmth of Sawyer's blood clinging to her trembling hands as she rose to her feet, her breath steady despite the storm of thoughts swirling in her mind.

Her focus remained on the sniper's nest, where she'd seen that glint off the scope. It was empty now, a phantom spot in the landscape. The shooter was gone, disappeared with the same precision that had taken Nathan Sawyer's life.

"He's gone," she finally said, her voice flat, devoid of emotion. She wiped her hands on her pants, the blood smearing more than cleaning. "And you've got yourself a sniper."

The sheriff's bewilderment exposed his lack of experience in such matters. "A sniper?"

"The shot was too clean, too precise. High-powered rifle. Not some random handgun fired from the crowd." Her tone was clinical, matter of fact. "It echoed off the rocks—long-range, from high ground. A sniper always picks the highest vantage point for visibility and distance."

She pointed with a blood-smeared finger toward the rocky cliffs looming beyond the parking lot, visible through the glass door. "I caught a scope glint up there just before the shot."

The sheriff followed her gesture, his face hardening. He yanked his radio from his belt and barked orders that cut through the chaos. "All units, possible sniper on the cliff! Set a perimeter, now! Move the crowd back and tell that ambulance to get here five minutes ago!"

The radio crackled in response, but Hatch had already tuned it out and turned away from the lifeless body on the ground. Sawyer was beyond saving. Every second wasted was another the sniper used to vanish deeper into the landscape, slipping further from reach.

She wiped her hands again, the crimson stains still clinging to her skin as a reminder of the life just lost. She worked at piecing together the fragments of the scene—the precision of the shot, the chaos that followed, and Sawyer's final word: *Maggie*. It echoed in her head, a riddle she couldn't yet solve.

The sheriff rose to his feet, his eyes narrowing as he sized her up. "Where do you think you're going?" His tone was authoritative, but the uncertainty lingered beneath it.

Hatch locked on the cliffs. "To find your sniper."

"Like hell you are," the sheriff snapped, his hand waving toward the disorder outside. But his voice held a tremor. "You leave that to my deputies."

Hatch glanced through the glass door. Two deputies wrestled to control the surging crowd, their shouts swallowed by the noise. Another struggled with a barricade, buckling under the pressure of panicked bodies.

"Your men are overwhelmed," Hatch said, her voice low, steady. "Every minute we waste, your shooter gets further away." She paused, meeting his eyes. "I've hunted people like this before. Let me do what I do best."

The sheriff's jaw tightened, indecision warring across his face. He opened his mouth to speak, but Hatch didn't wait for a blessing. "Jurisdiction won't matter when that sniper takes another shot. I'll report back if I find anything."

"Wait—I didn't catch your name?" the sheriff called after her, a mix of frustration and grudging respect coloring his voice.

Hatch pushed through the door without another word. Then she was gone.

THIRTEEN

HATCH SLICED THROUGH THE CROWD AS THE SHERIFF'S DEPUTIES SHOUTED at the protesters to disperse. She barely noticed the scattered glances thrown her way, the blood staining her clothes an afterthought compared to the mission at hand. Her focus remained locked on the rocky outcropping looming ahead, its dark silhouette cutting a jagged line into the overcast sky.

The earth squelched beneath her boots, still slick from the morning's rain. Ominous clouds choked the light, casting the world in shades of gray. The damp scent of pine and wet soil mingled with the metallic tang of blood.

Hatch moved with purpose, her eyes constantly scanning. The rugged terrain of the White Mountains stretched before her, a labyrinth of jagged hills and thick underbrush. She knew this kind of terrain well. It could either hide you or expose you. The sniper could have chosen any number of vantage points, but she had a hunch where to look.

A barely visible path appeared ahead, half-buried by wet leaves and debris. Without hesitation, Hatch began her ascent. Each step was a fight against gravity and the treacherous incline. The ground slid underfoot, slick with mud and loose stones. She'd slipped twice already, her body lurching as her boots skidded out from under her. Her palms scraped against the rough rocks, but she pushed on, the urgency of her mission overriding any discomfort.

Her breathing was controlled, steady, despite her pulse hammering in her ears. The wind picked up, whistling through the trees, carrying with it the distant rumble of an approaching storm. The higher she climbed, the more exposed she felt. Up here, the sniper could still be watching. Waiting.

At last, she reached the top, muscles aching from the effort. Instinctively, her hand slid to her Glock, drawing it from its holster and keeping it low. The landscape was sparse—scattered boulders and scraggly bushes, offering little in the way of cover. Hatch moved slowly, her senses on high alert. Every rustle of leaves, every shift in the wind, could be the prelude to an attack.

She approached the sniper's roost, scanning the area with the practiced eye of someone who had seen too many scenes like this. The ground was disturbed—patches of trampled grass, a few overturned stones. But the shooter had taken care, erasing most signs of their presence. Whoever had been here was skilled, disciplined. No rookie would leave a site this clean.

Hatch crouched, running her fingers over the damp earth, searching for anything that might have been missed in the sniper's haste. Then, beneath a pile of wet leaves, something caught her eye. A faint glint of silver. She leaned closer, peeling back the foliage to reveal a crumpled candy wrapper. An ordinary piece of trash, out of place here. Left behind by mistake.

She straightened, her thumb running over the wrapper's edge as her mind worked through the implications. The sniper had been careful, meticulous. Yet this wrapper hinted at a human flaw.

Her thoughts were interrupted by a sharp crack—the unmistakable sound of a stick snapping underfoot.

Hatch went still, her muscles tensing, eyes narrowing. The soft thud of deliberate footsteps followed, muffled by the wet ground. Someone was coming.

Her grip tightened on the Glock, her pulse quickening even as her breathing remained steady. She slowly turned toward the sound, her mind racing through possibilities. Was it one of the sheriff's men? Or was the sniper returning to cover their tracks?

Her senses sharpened, picking up every nuance—the faint scent of gun oil, the shift in the breeze as it carried the scent toward her. The stranger was approaching cautiously, likely aware that something was out of place.

With practiced calm, Hatch slipped behind a nearby boulder, using its bulk for cover. She moved smoothly, navigating the landscape, barely disturbing the air around her. From here, she had a clear view of the path but remained concealed, her Glock steady in her hand.

The footsteps slowed, a pause that told Hatch they were hesitating. They were alert, sensing danger.

She crouched lower, her breath quiet, her body poised for action. The cautious, deliberate footsteps resumed, closing in. A shadow flickered at the edge of her vision.

Any second now, the threat would round the boulder.

THE CRUNCH of a footstep had Hatch raising her Glock in an instant, her body coiled, ready for whatever emerged. But as the figure stepped from behind the rock, she recognized the sheriff's broad frame. She lowered her weapon, but her eyes continued their sweep, every nerve still on high alert.

The sheriff stumbled to a stop beside a gnarled pine, his breath ragged as he leaned on the tree, sweat glistening on his brow. "Used to run these mountains as a kid," he wheezed, a rueful grin pulling at his lips. "Now I get winded just walking up 'em." He chuckled, trying to catch his breath as his eyes appraised her, sharper than before.

"Shouldn't sneak up on someone like that. Not after what just happened."

"Didn't seem like I caught you off guard." He jutted his chin toward the gun bootlegged along her pantleg. "You find anything?"

Hatch pointed toward the disturbed ground. " He was set up over there."

The sheriff squinted, moving with slow, deliberate steps. He crouched, inspecting the site, doubt furrowing his brow. "You sure? I don't see much."

Hatch knelt beside him, her hands brushing the earth with practiced ease. "He used the local brush to cover his tracks," she explained, her voice calm. "Swept the dirt clean. Pro move. But no matter how good you are, you always leave something if you know where to look."

The sheriff gave her a sidelong glance, a mix of curiosity and grudging admiration in his tone. "Military?"

"Used to be," Hatch replied.

"What branch?"

"Army."

"I did a stint in the Army too. Years back." He slowly stood with a grimace, rubbing his knee. "Wanted to be a lifer, but a torn ligament on a jump changed my mind."

"Overseas?"

"No. Training at Benning. Never got my wings. But like my drill sergeant used to say, grunts don't need wings. We're earth pigs."

"You do any time in the sandbox?"

"One tour. Iraq." He eyed Hatch and then took a second look at the ground. "Never learned this kinda stuff, though."

Hatch shrugged, continuing her scan of their surroundings. "I guess it depends on the unit."

"Guess so." His arms akimbo. "Didn't catch your name back there."

"Hatch," she told him. "Just Hatch.

"Okay, Just Hatch." He arched his back, stretching and twisting to work out the kinks. "How do we go about tracking someone who doesn't leave tracks?"

Hatch stood and dusted off her hands. Sawyer's dried blood mixed with the dirt, leaving her skin in a smear of rust tones. "No one vanishes without a trace. Not even this guy. We just have to look at it from the right angle."

Something caught her eye. She crouched again, pushing aside damp leaves to reveal the crumpled fireball candy wrapper. "Like this."

The sheriff leaned closer, squinting his eyes. "You're telling me this is our big break?"

"Something's better than nothing," Hatch said. "Maybe he left some DNA, a partial print. If you're lucky, a bloodhound might pick up the scent."

The sheriff eyed her for a moment. "What exactly did you say you did in the Army?"

"I didn't." Less was more when it came to exposure. But if she planned to gain trust from the local lawman, she needed to open up a little. "Spent some time with the MPs. Worked in investigations before moving on."

"You're sure a jack of all trades."

"Not really." She squinted at the plastic square, careful not to touch it and contaminate any potential evidence.

He tugged his radio from his belt. "Dispatch, get me the state police. I'm gonna need their crime scene unit, ASAP."

"Will do," was the response. "Where would you like them to meet you?"

"Best to have them come to the resort. I'll guide them from there."

The sheriff looked to Hatch. "I'm gonna need you at the station later. After I get this shitshow under control, I'd like a full statement about the shooting. Maybe pick your brain some more on this shooter we're looking for."

"Sure thing," Hatch replied, already shifting her focus back. Her eyes scanned the rugged terrain ahead.

The sheriff stood beside her, following her gaze with his own. "What're you thinking?"

She pointed toward the dense expanse of the forest, its thick cover leading away from the hotel. "Your sniper's likely heading that way."

His brow furrowed. "Why that way?"

She shrugged. "That's where I'd go."

FOURTEEN

THE CHAOS HAD FINALLY SETTLED, BUT UNEASE LINGERED LIKE A MIST, thick and pervasive. Evelyn Hartwell stood near the parking lot, clutching Chloe's hand as though it could anchor her in the aftermath. The echo of the gunshot still reverberated in her mind.

Most of the protesters had dispersed, leaving only a few onlookers casting wary glances toward the yellow crime scene tape that fluttered in the wind. It was a quiet Evelyn had never wanted to associate with fear, but now it clung to the day, unsettling and heavy.

Chloe, always so full of life, was still as a statue, her wide eyes staring at the police cars and the tape, trying to make sense of what had unfolded. The earlier excitement of attending the rally had dissolved, leaving only fear. Evelyn squeezed her daughter's hand tighter, wishing she could absorb the terror radiating from her little girl, protect her from the ugly reality that had shattered their day.

Nearby, Liam hovered like a guardian, his lanky frame taut with tension. His eyes, sharp for his age, swept the area, constantly vigilant. He wasn't Evelyn's son, but Liam had taken on the role of Chloe's protector. The way he looked out for her filled Evelyn with both pride and sadness. He'd grown up too fast, forced to bear burdens far beyond his years.

Evelyn's attention drifted to Sheriff Tuck, who stood at the base of the rocky cliff, deep in conversation with one of his deputies. The set of his shoulders, the tightness in his face, told her more than any words could. This was no routine disturbance. Whatever had happened today, it was far from over. She could see it in the way he gestured toward the ridge, the way his posture carried the weight of something darker, something that wouldn't be easily resolved.

"Mom." Chloe's soft voice, fragile and trembling, pulled Evelyn from her thoughts. "Can we go home now?"

Crouching down, Evelyn brushed a lock of hair from Chloe's face, forcing a smile that she hoped would provide some comfort. "Yes, sweetie. We'll leave soon. Everything's going to be okay." But as she said it, the words felt hollow.

Liam stepped forward, placing a protective hand on Chloe's shoulder, his voice steady despite the tension surrounding them. "I'll take her to the car."

"Thank you, Liam," Evelyn murmured, her gratitude tinged with exhaustion.

She watched as Liam gently guided Chloe to the old station wagon, never letting go of her. The sight filled Evelyn with a bittersweet ache— pride in the boy Liam was becoming, but sorrow for the innocence he and Chloe had lost today. They shouldn't have to shoulder this kind of weight. Not yet. But she was deeply grateful for Liam's strength. Especially now.

The sheriff's approach pulled her attention back to the scene. His face was etched with lines of worry and the unspoken burden, the lines she'd come to recognize when something serious weighed on him.

"You should take Chloe home," he said quietly, his voice firm but not without gentleness. "She needs to get some rest after all this."

Evelyn nodded and studied his face for a moment, searching for the answers he couldn't yet give. "What about you?"

"I've got things to finish up here. This is … more than we thought."

Liam, having reached the car and helping Chloe inside, walked back toward them. Concern was etched on his young face. "You want me to drive them home, Dad?"

A sense of pride warmed him. Liam was becoming the man Tuck hoped him to be, maybe more so. "No, son. Just follow them. Make sure they get there safe."

Liam hesitated, clearly wanting to offer more, but he held back. "Got it."

As the sheriff returned to his duties, Evelyn felt the familiar twinge in her chest—a complicated mix of concern and something deeper, unspoken. Their relationship had always teetered on the edge of something more, yet neither had taken that next step. Watching him now, his shoulders weighed down with strain, made her want to reach out, to help him carry the burden.

"Your dad's going to be okay, right?" she asked, turning to Liam.

Liam didn't answer immediately. "He's always okay. He's tough as they come."

But Evelyn knew better. She had seen that look in the sheriff's eyes before, a man who recognized danger and wouldn't back down from it. Whatever lay ahead, it wasn't going to be simple, and the ripple effects would touch them all.

She climbed in the car and pulled away. In the rearview mirror, the crime scene shrank into the distance, the fluttering yellow tape serving as a reminder of how dramatically her small world had been turned upside down. Evelyn's grip tightened on the steering wheel as the old station wagon descended the mountain road.

FIFTEEN

HIS FINGERS ADJUSTED THE BINOCULARS WITH SURGICAL PRECISION. HE watched the woman descending the ridge, her movements a symphony of efficiency and purpose. He'd caught a glimpse of her the previous night at the hotel, a fleeting shadow that had lodged in his memory like a splinter. Something about her set his teeth on edge, a quality that spoke of shared dark spaces and unspoken horrors.

She moved with fluid precision. Every step, every glance, tactical.

Who the hell is she?

The question gnawed at him, burrowing deep. She wasn't part of the senator's usual detail—he knew them all, had their routines committed to memory. This woman? An unknown. Her mere existence was enough to set off alarms in his head.

He stowed the binoculars with practiced efficiency. No need to linger. The sniper's nest was clean, wiped of any trace. She wouldn't find so much as a hair, but her presence alone spelled trouble. And in his world, trouble had a nasty habit of snowballing.

Moving deeper into the dense woods, his body slipped through the trees with fluid grace. This was his element—silent, invisible, lethal. The forest embraced him, its canopy shielding him from prying eyes. Underbrush swallowed his tracks, leaving no trace. He moved quickly, but carefully. Walking heal-to-toe with each measured step.

The extraction point was just a few clicks northeast. The path was etched in his mind, every choke point and escape route catalogued. He had taken the shot, played his part. Now it was time to disappear, to become nothing more than a whisper on the wind.

A shallow stream cut through his path, gurgling softly. He stepped across the rocks, careful not to disturb the water. No tracks, no signs. Just one more thread in his vanishing act.

The ground sloped into a narrow ravine. Descending with the grace of a cat, his boots barely touched the soft earth. As he neared the clearing, his senses heightened. Wind rustled the leaves, carrying with it the faintest hint of a storm on the horizon.

He crouched low, sweeping the area with a practiced eye. Satisfied, he pulled out his radio, thumb pressing the call button. His voice was low, controlled. "Requesting extract. Over."

Nothing. Silence.

Bishop frowned, checked the signal. Full bars. He keyed the mic again, this time with more bite in his voice. "Extract. Now. Over."

Dead air. The silence pressed in, thick and heavy.

A chill coiled around his spine, the hair on his neck standing at attention. Something was off. He didn't bother with a third call. Third chances were for amateurs.

The extraction point was compromised.

His mind shifted, cycling through contingencies. *Plan Bravo—head for the alternate exfil site two clicks south, using the ravine for cover. If that's blown, fallback to the safe house. If pursuit engages, prioritize evasion and delay contact until I'm on better ground.* The radio disappeared into his vest as he scanned the tree line, his eyes narrowing on every shadow and movement.

This had to be a setup.

Bishop adjusted his rifle strap, rolling his shoulders to stay loose. He didn't move yet. Instead, he dropped lower, slipping into the underbrush, his footsteps muffled against the damp earth. *First rule of survival —don't make yourself a target.*

He moved, quick but controlled. Northwest, toward the secondary rendezvous. There was always a backup plan. Always. He had outmaneuvered death on three continents, survived alone in enemy territory with nothing but his wits and a combat knife. This was no different. His instincts were screaming at him now, honed through countless operations where failure meant death.

The radio silence wasn't a glitch. It was deliberate. Calculated.

They weren't just abandoning him. Cutting him loose.

Bishop's pace quickened, but his breathing remained steady. His mind processed the implications, but his body was already moving. He'd been burned before. He knew the game. There was no loyalty here, no fairytales about a clean getaway. The moment he became a liability, they were the ones to pull the trigger.

The wind shifted, rustling the leaves, carrying the scent of rain. His muscles coiled, ready to spring into action.

Disappearing was his specialty. But this time, it would be on his terms.

He pressed deeper into the woods, his mind sharp, calculating. One thought crystallized: survive. Always on his terms.

SIXTEEN

Hatch moved through the underbrush, eyes constantly roving, cataloging every detail. The forest pressed in around her, the muted light filtering through the canopy casting the world in shades of green and gray. Damp earth clung to her boots, the scent of pine and rain thick in the air. She blocked it all out, her mind zeroed in on the task at hand.

A snapped twig caught her eye, its sharp angle betraying a hurried passage. She crouched, fingers brushing the soil, feeling the faint impression of a boot print. Barely there, but enough.

Gotcha.

The sniper was fast, experienced. But even the best made mistakes when the clock was ticking. The depth of the print, the angle—it all told a story. Hatch read it like a book. This wasn't just a run. This was a controlled retreat.

She stood and continued, every step deliberate. The forest seemed to hold its breath, waiting for what came next. Her senses sharpened, attuned to the subtle rhythms of the land. A low-hanging branch had been snapped. The first sign, a careless mistake, forced by the pressure of the hunt. Her lips twitched into something that wasn't quite a smile.

Every mistake is another's opportunity. Something her dad drilled into her head. Something that had driven her to perfection, or at the very least, her relentless pursuit of it.

The murmur of water drew her attention, the rushing sound growing louder as she reached the edge of a swollen stream. The current was fast, angry, carving through the earth like a knife. The trail vanished at the bank, the footprints dissolving into nothing.

Hatch paused, eyes scanning the far side of the stream. If she were him, she'd use the water to wash away the tracks, make herself invisible. A fallen log slick with rain and moss half-submerged in the current would be a natural crossing point.

Smart.

Her fingers drummed against her thigh as she weighed her options. She could cross, take the risk, but the stream was treacherous. And if she was wrong, she'd lose time. Her eyes flicked up and down the banks. There were no signs the sniper had made it across, but then again, someone that skilled wouldn't leave signs easily.

Her phone buzzed, the sudden sound breaking the silence. She didn't need to look to know who it was.

"Where are you?" Reeves' voice crackled through the line, sharp, clipped.

"Tracking the shooter," Hatch said, eyes still on the water. "I've got a potential lead."

"I need you back here." A pause, then Reeves' tone hardened. "We need to regroup. The senator is the principal. Let law enforcement handle the investigation."

Hatch's jaw clenched. The trail was getting cold, and the sniper was slipping away. She could feel it, like sand running through her fingers. She hated leaving things unfinished, especially something like this. She reminded herself of what Tracy had said, about this being the opportunity to clear the stink off them from Arizona. Stirring the pot would only serve to complicate things. And whether or not she wholly agreed, Reeves was right. The senator is the assignment.

Hatch exhaled slowly. She gave the stream one last look, committing to memory the area around the crossing. She pulled a folding knife from her pocket and carved an X into a nearby tree. If she had the opportunity to resume her search, at least she'd have a starting point.

"On my way."

She collapsed the knife and clipped it back inside her pocket before turning her back to the rushing water. Her boots sank into the mud as she started down the trail. The sniper had been good. The shot, the escape—it all spoke of someone with serious training. Someone like her.

But no one was perfect. He'd left a trace, regardless of how small. And mistakes could be capitalized on. If given the chance, she planned to do just that.

HATCH'S BOOTS squelched on the plush carpet as she entered the senator's quarters, the mud and dried blood caking her pants stark against the room's polished luxury. The air was thick, too warm after the damp chill of the forest. The scent of whiskey mixed with rich wood polish, and the faint sound of classical music hummed from a turntable in the corner.

Hatch had experienced this juxtaposition before, upon returning to base after some of her more harrowing missions. Entering the mess hall to the jocularity of those at the FOB always served as a jolt into a different reality. She felt it here now.

Reeves glanced at her, eyes narrowing at the sight of her disheveled state. "While you were skipping through the forest," he said, voice tight, "we've been trying to figure out what the hell went wrong."

Hatch clenched her jaw tight. Skipping through the forest? Right. She hadn't been wading through mud and chasing down a sniper for her own amusement. She opened her mouth to fire back, but Senator Masterson's voice cut through, smooth as the whiskey in his hand.

"Drink?" Masterson offered. He held up his empty tumbler, the ice rattling in the glass.

She declined with a simple shake of her head. Masterson ambled over to the counter, pouring himself three fingers worth of the amber liquid from a crystal decanter. Something about his movements seemed off to Hatch. He was steady, too controlled for a man who'd just had a sniper's crosshairs on him hours ago.

Velvet drapes, mahogany furniture, thick carpet underfoot. It felt suffocating, like all the life had been drained out of the air, leaving only polished surfaces and false comfort.

"Sir, I think we need to take a hard look at this threat. I don't think we're dealing with some deranged lunatic here."

"Maybe we should be discussing your tactics." Reeves leaned against the back wall with crossed arms.

"Come again?" Hatch nearly launched across the room. She fought the urge. Her face reddened under the strain.

"If you'd been paying more attention out there, maybe you'd have spotted the shooter before—"

"Now, now," Masterson said, swirling the whiskey in his hand. "We're all on the same side here. Everything happened so fast. I don't think pointing the finger is going to do us any good."

HATCH SAID NOTHING. Her eyes remained locked on Reeves.

"Senator's right." He shot her a conciliatory look. "Just still trying to wrap my head around it all."

"Then maybe you should've let me continue tracking our shooter." Hatch's voice was clipped. "I warned you about the guy I saw in the hotel last night. My guess would be that he's got something to do with this."

"Maybe. I already forwarded the information to the sheriff. Best we leave the work of it to him and his men. Our focus is protection." Reeves pushed off the wall and stepped into the center of the room. "For starters, we need to determine the existing threat and how to best protect the senator going forward."

"Change the itinerary, for one. If he is the intended target, might be a good idea to take a detour from the campaign trail."

"No way I'm going to let some nut job take me off the path to re-election." Masterson plunked himself into the soft leather seat. "Too much riding on this. I back down now, there'll be no coming back."

"And what do you mean by *if?*" Reeves asked. "You think that the shooter wasn't taking aim at the senator?"

Hatch shrugged. "Got to look at it from all possible angles."

"You're trying to tell me that a sniper was looking to pick off the senator's underling?" Reeves tossed his hands up. "Why in the world would Sawyer be a target? He's a nobody."

"Let's not speak ill of the dead. Sawyer was a good man. A loyal campaign manager. Someone I trusted." Masterson raised his glass as if punctuating his remark with a toast.

Hatch took notice of the senator's hand. Not a tremor. His calm could be the result of the libation sedation he was using to self-medicate, but it was still out of place. In her world, when something didn't fit, you peeled back the layers until it did.

Most people—even the trained ones—would have shown some kind of crack. A tremor. A nervous glance. Not Masterson. He looked like he was enjoying this, like it was all just some game to him. Her instincts flared. Something dangerous simmered beneath his easy demeanor.

She kept her tone casual as she asked, "You ever serve, Senator?"

"In the military?" Masterson raised an eyebrow, his eyes taking on a glossy sheen. "Me? No, never had the pleasure. Politics was my battlefield. Business too." He sipped the whiskey. "Different kind of war, I suppose. Why do you ask?"

"You've got the nerves of a combat vet," Hatch mused, gesturing with a nod of her head. "Steady hands."

Something flickered behind Masterson's eyes. "Politics can be ... cutthroat. And the bourbon helps."

Hatch nodded but didn't buy it. She'd seen men under fire lose their composure faster than this. His calm felt rehearsed, like a mask that didn't quite fit. She filed it away, the picture of the senator growing more complicated by the second.

Hatch debated her next move. Deciding that reading the room's reaction would give her insight, she decided to lay her cards on the table. "One more question, Senator. The name 'Maggie' mean anything to you?"

Masterson frowned, the first real sign of confusion crossing his face. "Maggie? No, can't say it does. Why?"

Maybe it was genuine confusion—or maybe it was just good practice.

"Just something Sawyer said before he died."

Masterson looked to Reeves. *"Does the name ring a bell?"*

"Never heard mention of her before. Maybe it was a girlfriend or something. I can look into it."

"You do that." Masterson sipped slowly.

A knock interrupted them. Masterson's aide—barely old enough to have a driver's license—poked his head in, looking nervous. "Senator, Sheriff Tuck called. He would like to set a time to get statements about today's shooting. Apparently, he needs to debrief everyone. Including you, sir."

"Reeves will take care of the arrangements." Masterson sighed, setting his glass down with a deliberate clink. He adjusted his tie, standing up with the grace of a man who hadn't just been hunted by a sniper. His face morphed, setting aside the tension, the practiced ease returning. "Duty calls. I've got to get ready for a press conference."

"Why don't you head over to meet with the sheriff?" Reeves tossed Hatch a set of keys. "Take the Tahoe. Might as well have a set of wheels while you're here."

Hatch caught the keys midair. "Sure thing. Just going to wash up first."

"And Hatch, let's not go sharing theories with the locals until we've got a better understanding of what's going on here."

"That an order?"

"Consider it a friendly suggestion."

Hatch saw nothing friendly in Reeves' eyes as she turned to leave.

SEVENTEEN

THE WATER RAN CLEAR, BUT HATCH'S HANDS STILL FELT STICKY. SHE scrubbed harder, knuckles raw as the cheap motel soap barely lathered. The majority of Sawyer's blood was gone, but remnants stubbornly clung to her skin—a visceral reminder of everything that had gone wrong.

She killed the tap. Drip. Drip. Drip. The sound echoed in the small, dingy bathroom like the metronome of her racing thoughts. *Why hadn't I seen it coming?* The question hammered at her skull. *The signs were there —the bottleneck in the hallway, the way the crowd shifted. I should've anticipated the ambush.*

She stared at her reflection in the cracked mirror. Her eyes were hollow, face drawn. *Sawyer's dead because I was seconds too slow.* Her jaw tightened as she gripped the edge of the sink, the cheap porcelain cool under her fingers. *I should've forced him tighter to the protection detail.*

The faint tang of iron lingered in her nostrils, no matter how many times she inhaled. *Once that bullet found its mark, there was nothing to do. Too much blood. Too fast. Even if I'd gotten him out faster, it wouldn't have made a difference.* The rational part of her knew all of this. But rationality offered little comfort when the weight of failure pressed down like a vice.

Her gaze dropped to her hands. Faint pink stains around her finger-nails caught in the yellowish light. Anger swelled to meet her guilt.

The dripping tap punctuated the silence again. Drip. Drip. Drip. Hatch clenched her fists, staring at the water pooling in the basin. *It's not over. The people who set this in motion are still out there.* She straightened, her reflection hardening in the mirror. *I won't let this be for nothing.*

Her bloodstained clothes hit the trash with a wet thud. Not the first time she'd tossed evidence, but this felt different. Heavier. She pulled on fresh layers, the cool fabric soothing against her raw skin, but it did little to ease the weight pressing down on her.

The phone buzzed from the nightstand.

Tracy's voice came through, low and steady. "Tell me everything."

Hatch didn't waste time. "Sniper took a shot. Senator's still breathing, but his campaign manager, Nathan Sawyer, is not. Single round, center mass. He bled out fast."

A beat of silence. "That went to shit fast. So much for an easy in and out."

"I need you to do some digging into Sawyer. Not sure what's going on here."

"Why?" No judgement in the question. Unlike Reeves.

"Call it intuition. It wasn't an easy shot. Distance, windage would all play a factor. Plus, the protective detail was tight to the senator."

"Sounds like a professional."

"Exactly. Not to mention, the spot where the shot was taken was wiped clean. His track was too."

"What are you getting at?"

"One shot, from what I would guess is a highly trained individual. Doubt he'd miss. And if he did, why not place another?" Hatch replayed the scene in her mind. "My gut's telling me he didn't miss."

"Making Sawyer the intended target."

"Just a theory."

"Worth running down." Tracy paused. "Maybe this Sawyer guy was mixed up with the wrong people."

"Possibly."

"You don't sound convinced."

"It just doesn't add up. Why make it look like a botched assassination attempt? Seems like a whole lot of effort for someone Reeves described as a *nobody*."

"Agreed. You've got a proven track record of following your gut. What's it telling you?"

"That something's amiss." Hatch thought of the dying declaration. "One more thing. Just before he died, Sawyer said a name. Maggie."

"Anyone there know what the connection might be?"

"No. Reeves figured maybe a girlfriend."

"But you don't agree?"

"I don't know enough to form an opinion. It's something worth checking into."

"You do remember you're there as part of the protective detail, not as an investigator?"

"What'd you do, speak with Reeves?" There was an edge to her voice, one she made no attempt at hiding.

Tracy sighed. "Let me guess, you're applying your special talent for pissing off people?"

"Just callin' it like I see it."

"This time I'd have to agree. He's right about steering clear and letting the local police do their job."

"I'm not here to rock the boat. Just want to make sure this shooter doesn't get away. Besides, I've got a meeting with the sheriff in a little bit. Should have a good idea on how things are being handled after that."

"Keep me posted."

"Do me a favor, let me know if you can make any connections between Sawyer and this Maggie person." Hatch hesitated. "There's one more thing. Guy at the hotel last night. Didn't belong. Not security. Not local. My guess is he's tied to this. Might even be our shooter."

Another pause. Then, a rustle, and Banyan's voice cut in. "Need me to saddle up and head out?"

Hatch smirked, though her mind stayed sharp. "Hate to pull you from that cushy desk job."

"Cushy, my ass," Banyan shot back, but Hatch could hear the eagerness. "You good?"

"I'm fine. Nothing I can't handle. But I'm about as welcome here as a skunk at a garden party."

Banyan chuckled. "When's that ever stopped you?"

"Point taken."

"We'll look into it," Tracy said. "I'll brief the General. Gauge his thoughts on all this."

"If I have any say, I'd like to see this through."

"Remember, we're on thin ice. Playing by the rules this time 'round."

"Copy that."

A beat of silence stretched between them, then Tracy said, "Watch your six out there."

"Always do," Hatch replied before ending the call.

Pocketing her phone, Hatch stepped back out of the motel room and into the Chevy. The silhouette of the mountains in the backdrop as she pulled out of the lot. The shooter was out there somewhere, slipping through the night like water through a sieve.

———

HATCH PULLED into the visitor's lot at the sheriff's office. Just as she was about to exit the vehicle, her phone vibrated. It was Tracy again. She answered it on the second ring.

"That was quick. What'd you find?"

"Still working on Sawyer's connection to all of this. Nothing yet on Maggie."

"Then what's up? Am I getting recalled?" Hatch was about to go on the offensive, defending her actions on scene, fearful that Reeves had forwarded his assessment of her with less than favorable remarks.

"No," Tracy replied, voice laced with amusement. "In fact, you're being reassigned to assist in the manhunt. We've got a lead on who the shooter is."

"That was fast."

"Things are evolving quickly."

"You said I was being reassigned." Hatch thought about the resistance by Reeves up to this point. "Reassigned by who?"

"Thorne. He said you're likely the only one capable of tracking this guy down."

Hatch was silent for a moment. "The General said those words?"

"Not exactly, but it was implied."

"Why the sudden change of heart?"

"I guess he's under pressure to bring this to resolution. Not convinced the locals are equipped to handle it."

"We still don't even know who the shooter is. Or who the intended target was."

"For the time being, let's assume it was the senator. If evidence leads elsewhere, we can deal with it as it comes to light."

"Fair enough." Hatch looked at the small office housing the local police force and knew this situation was well beyond their expertise.

"We're making arrangements for you to assist the sheriff. You'll be privy to anything gleaned from the investigation thus far, as well as having their assets at your disposal."

"I'm sure that'll go over well."

"There's something else." Tracy let the silence settle between them before speaking again. "I just learned that there's apparently been an operation underway here to bring in one of ours who's gone off the reservation."

"You're saying one of our people has gone rogue?" Hatch dropped the volume of her voice to a whisper, even though she was alone in the vehicle. "And this is our shooter?"

"Looks that way. Still getting read in on all of this."

"Read in? Thought you were cleared to the top."

"There's always someone above. In this case, that's Thorne."

"Makes sense now why he'd want to me to go after him. Containment."

"It also goes without saying that the General would like to minimize any exposure to Talon itself."

"Understood. So, what do we know about our guy?"

"His name is Kyle Bishop. I'm sending you a file with his picture."

Hatch felt the vibration alert for the incoming message. She took a second to open the attachment and study the image. The file was a dated DA photo from his time in service. It was a younger, cleaner cut of the man she'd seen the other night sitting at the chess table. But the rugged jawline and build were the same.

"That's him. That's the guy I saw in the hotel last night. Photo's a bit dated, but I can say without a doubt, this is the guy who gave me the slip." Hatch expanded her fingers across the image, zooming in on the Bishop's face. "Any intel?"

Tracy's voice lowered. "Most of his file's been redacted. I've got Banyan trying to do some digging. From what I've been briefed, Bishop is one of Talon's most lethal assets. He has carried out several operations with an unprecedented mission success rate."

"Maybe Talon should be sending some more men this way."

"Thorne's putting together a standby team. Your job is asset containment."

"Containment?"

"Find him. Once located, there'll be a team on the ground to handle the rest." Tracy exhaled. "He's dangerous. Knows the tricks of the trade. Watch your step."

Hatch took one more look at the man she'd been tasked with bringing in. "I'm at the station now. Burning daylight. I'll link up with the sheriff and get this hunt underway."

She hung up, grabbing her jacket from the passenger seat. The weight of her Glock in its holster brought a sense of calm, its cold, familiar metal against her side. She did a quick press check, making sure it was in battery. With a guy like Bishop, there'd be no room for error.

The temperature had begun a nosedive. She stepped outside and zipped her jacket, trapping what little heat she could as her breath formed clouds in the crisp air as she made her way to the station.

EIGHTEEN

THE AROMA OF SIMMERING BEEF AND VEGETABLES FILLED THE COZY kitchen, blending with the fading light of the evening. Evelyn Hartwell stirred the pot, occasionally checking out of the window. Outside, the sun was sinking behind the pine trees, casting long shadows that reached across the room, the warm, muted glow of twilight settling in. It was peaceful here, nestled in the foothills, where the world seemed far away.

Today's events shattered that illusion.

Evelyn glanced over at Chloe, who sat quietly at the worn oak table, her chin resting in her palms as she watched Liam shuffle a deck of cards. He had insisted on following them home after the incident, his protective instincts in overdrive. Now, he was keeping Chloe entertained while Evelyn prepped dinner, providing a much-needed distraction.

As she turned back to the stove, Evelyn's gaze landed on the blood sugar monitor resting on the counter. She'd checked Chloe's levels only a few minutes ago. It was a subconscious habit born from fear. Her daughter had nearly died before the doctor had figured out her condition. She'd spent years blaming herself. She'd spend the rest of her life making sure her daughter was safe, a debt she planned to pay in full.

Her eyes flicked to Chloe, who giggled as Liam fumbled a card trick, her cheeks flushed with the carefree joy of a child.

Liam grinned, his fingers effortlessly moving through the cards. "Ever tried poker, Chloe?"

Chloe shook her head, her voice small. "I haven't."

Liam's grin widened, a chipped front tooth giving him an easy charm. "No problem. I'll teach you. Just don't let the sheriff know I'm corrupting you."

For the first time since they'd returned home, a smile tugged at Chloe's lips. She drummed her fingers lightly on the table. "It's just ... all this weird stuff happening, I'm tired of it." Her voice was quiet but steady. "But I'm glad you're here, Liam."

Liam reached over and ruffled her hair in a brotherly way. "You're tough, Chloe. You'll get through this. Trust me."

Evelyn glanced over her shoulder, a warmth spreading in her chest. It was good to see Chloe coming back to life, even if just for a moment. Liam's steady presence was like a lifeline, and Evelyn was grateful.

The phone rang, cutting through the peace. Evelyn wiped her hands on a dish towel and answered, already knowing who it would be.

"Ms. Hartwell? It's Dr. Hensley," came the familiar voice of her employer, the town veterinarian. "I hate to ask, but my mother took a bad fall. She's in the hospital and I need to go be with her. Do you mind closing up the clinic tonight? Just check on the animals, make sure everything's locked up?"

Evelyn hesitated, glancing at the bubbling stew, then at Chloe and Liam. It wasn't ideal, but Dr. Hensley had been good to her. This job kept her dream of someday attending veterinary school alive.

"Of course," Evelyn said, pushing down the reluctance. "I'll take care of everything. I hope your mom's okay."

"Thank you," Hensley replied, his relief palpable. "I owe you one."

She hung up, her mind already spinning. Dinner would have to wait, but the stew could simmer. She turned to Chloe. "Sweetheart, I need to head out for a bit. Just to check on things at the clinic."

Chloe's face fell, her disappointment clear. "Do you have to?"

Evelyn knelt beside her, brushing a lock of hair from Chloe's face.

"I'll be back before you know it. Liam's here, so you won't have to be alone."

Evelyn straightened and turned to Liam. "Would it be too much trouble for you to stick around until I get back?"

Liam, surprised but willing, said, "No trouble at all, Ms. Hartwell. I've got it."

Relief flooded through her. "Thanks. The stew just needs another hour. Turn off the burner when the timer goes off and move the pot off the heat. You two can go ahead and eat." She wiped her hands again, more out of habit than necessity, scanning the room to make sure everything was in order. "And Chloe, don't forget to brush your teeth before bed. I'll be back in time to tuck you in, okay?"

Chloe did her best to hide the disappointment. "Okay."

Evelyn leaned down and kissed her forehead. "I'll be quick."

Evelyn grabbed her jacket from the hook by the door and stepped out into the evening, the cool air wrapping around her like a cloak. The scent of pine and damp earth filled her senses as the night settled in. Their house sat on the edge of the foothills, far enough from town to feel remote but close enough for a sense of community. A small stream ran along the back of the property, its gurgling flow a constant companion to the quiet evenings. Tonight, though, the sound seemed louder, as if the world was holding its breath.

She made her way to the car, pausing for a moment to look back at the house. Warm light spilled from the kitchen window, illuminating the interior where Liam and Chloe were seated across from each other.

Evelyn climbed into the driver's seat, gripping the wheel as the engine rumbled to life. She couldn't shake the unease from earlier. The feeling clung to her. The incident at the hotel had rattled her in ways she wasn't ready to admit, and the thought of leaving Chloe—even with Liam there—gnawed at her.

But there was no avoiding it. Duty called. With the lapse in insurance, the extra hours on this week's paycheck would be a welcome addition. Her husband's life insurance policy had enabled her to pay down their mortgage. Otherwise, she wouldn't have been able to keep it going.

Now, Beauregard Covington was trying to take their home away. She pushed the thought from her mind.

The headlights cut through the gloom as Evelyn pulled onto the narrow road leading toward town. The darkness closed in around her, the quiet of the night pressing in, broken only by the hum of the engine. In the distance, the lights of the town twinkled faintly, barely visible through the trees.

A shiver ran down her spine as the feeling of being watched crept back in, a gnawing sensation she couldn't quite shake. The mountains seemed different tonight, less protective and more foreboding, as if they, too, were hiding secrets.

BISHOP CROUCHED in the shadow of a craggy outcropping, his eyes cutting through the mist-shrouded New Hampshire mountains. Rain fell in a steady, relentless sheet, soaking into his clothes despite every effort to stay dry. He'd been entrenched here for hours, hidden far from his abandoned vehicle, knowing the rugged terrain was his best chance to remain unseen. Leaving even the faintest trace in his line of work could mean the difference between vanishing into the night or ending up in a body bag.

Beneath the jagged rocks, Bishop had dug a shallow pit for his fire— a flicker of heat without smoke, a technique he'd perfected over years of survival. The flames were hot enough to cook the brook trout he'd caught earlier from a mountain stream, the scent of the fish barely detectable in the damp forest surrounding him. He had fashioned a crude spit from branches to cook it evenly, every action executed with quiet precision. For Bishop, survival wasn't just instinct. It was an art.

His jacket and boots lay near the pit, slowly drying in the meager heat. But the damp chill still gnawed at him, a reminder of his exposure to the elements. He barely noticed. Discomfort was an old companion, one he'd learned to embrace. He focused on his gear, sharpening his knife by the firelight. Each stroke was measured, each moment a preparation for the next move. The wilderness was his element. He could stay out here indefinitely, becoming part of the landscape whenever he needed to.

The sudden beep from his encrypted phone cut through the steady drum of rain. Bishop moved his hand with practiced speed, retrieving the device from his vest. The screen illuminated his face in the twilight gloom, casting sharp shadows across his scarred features.

No extract. Secondary target. Encrypted file sent.

Bishop's jaw tightened as he tapped the screen. A photograph materialized—a woman's face, partially obscured by shadow but clear enough to recognize. He stared at it for a long moment, his mind running through the implications. The mission had changed, and there was no room for hesitation.

NINETEEN

SHERIFF ROY TUCK STOOD AT THE FRONT OF THE CRAMPED BRIEFING room, his weathered hands resting on the scarred wooden podium. The fluorescent lights buzzed overhead, casting harsh shadows across the faces of his deputies. Tuck scanned over each of them, reading their readiness. They were all good people, salt of the earth, but none of them had ever dealt with a threat quite like this. The man they were after wasn't your run-of-the-mill criminal. Hatch had made that painfully clear.

"Listen up," Tuck said, his gravelly voice cutting through the thick, stale air. "We need to presume this guy is highly trained and extremely dangerous. This ain't some backwoods meth cook or a drunk driver. This is a whole different ballgame." He paused, locking eyes with each deputy, making sure they understood the gravity of the situation. "No one's playing hero here. I don't want anyone going off half-cocked thinking they can bring him in without backup. Am I clear?"

A round of, "Yes, sir," followed, but Tuck didn't miss the mix of excitement and unease in their expressions. It was the biggest thing to hit this sleepy town in years, and they all felt it.

Deputy Jackson, tall and wiry, with a sharp jawline to match his quick wit, raised his hand. His other hand absently petted his blood-hound, Rufus, who sat attentively at his feet. "Sheriff, I don't want to state the obvious, but how are we supposed to track this guy? We don't have a scent trail. No scent, no track." He glanced down at Rufus, whose ears twitched as if sensing the challenge ahead.

Tuck reached into his coat pocket and pulled out an evidence bag containing a crinkled Fireball candy wrapper. The red cellophane caught the dim light as he held it up. "Will this suffice, Jackson?"

Jackson leaned forward, squinting at the wrapper, then grinned, his eyes darting between Tuck and Rufus. "I'll be damned. This ol' boy here can track a gnat's fart in a field of manure. That wrapper's plenty."

A ripple of nervous laughter moved through the room. Tuck's expression turned serious again. He shot a glance out the window, where the late afternoon sun was sinking low, casting long shadows across the parking lot. Time was slipping away.

"We're losing daylight. I want to get a move on before nightfall. Rufus's our best shot at getting a trail before this guy vanishes."

One of the younger deputies, Sarah Chen, raised her hand. "Sheriff, if this guy's so dangerous, why's he still hanging around? Shouldn't he have skipped town by now?"

"Good point, Chen. My gut's telling me he's still here. Not sure the reason." He paused, brow furrowing. "Maybe he's tying up loose ends. Maybe he's waiting for something. Or someone. Either way, we need to find him before he disappears... or decides to make more trouble."

Jackson gave Rufus a reassuring pat, the bloodhound's ears perking up. "Ready when you are, Sheriff. Just give the word."

Tuck's gut tightened. Hatch's warning echoed in his mind. This wasn't a game. Every minute they weren't on this man's trail was another he could be slipping away or setting up for something deadly.

Tuck continued, his voice full of resolve. "We start now. I'll coordinate with the state police. Chen, you're with me. Jackson, you and Rufus take point on the ground. The rest of you, set up a perimeter. No one's going home until we have a lead."

He took one last look around the room, making sure to look every deputy in their eyes. "Let's find this bastard before he disappears."

HATCH STEPPED into the sheriff's office, the faint aroma of brewed coffee and old paper greeting her. The air was cool, the hum of an aging air conditioner blending with the occasional ring of a desk phone. The walls were lined with community bulletins, faded wanted posters, and a large corkboard pinned with maps and notes. Behind the front desk, a pleasant woman with short, graying hair looked up from her computer and offered a warm smile.

"You must be Hatch," the woman said, standing and extending a hand. "I'm Pearl. Welcome."

Hatch returned the handshake. "Nice to make your acquaintance, Pearl. The sheriff in?"

"Right this way." Pearl gestured toward a hallway at the back. "He's in the briefing room. You're just in time."

Hatch followed, her boots echoing faintly against the scuffed tile floor. As she approached the doorway, she heard the sheriff's voice—a steady baritone delivering the final details of an operational plan. She lingered for a moment in the hallway, catching bits of his instructions about patrol rotations and crowd control.

When she stepped inside, the deputies were rising from their chairs, hats in hand, preparing to clear out. The room was utilitarian, with a rectangular table at its center, a whiteboard covered in scribbled notes on one wall, and a bulletin board peppered with photographs and maps on another.

The sheriff looked up at her entrance.

"Well, well, if it ain't our new liaison," Tuck greeted, his voice just loud enough for Hatch to hear. "Guess you've got some friends in high places."

"Seems so." Hatch met his outstretched hand with a firm grip. "I was advised to lend a hand where I could."

His voice cut through the room. "Hold up, folks. Take your seats."

The deputies exchanged glances before settling back down, their curiosity evident as their eyes flicked toward Hatch.

"Gentlemen, I'd like you to meet Hatch," the sheriff said, stepping forward. "She's here to assist with our efforts. You'll want to hear what she has to say."

"Not here to take over. Just to help capture this guy as quickly and safely as possible,"

Hatch said. "The man we're after isn't just skilled—he's elite. Disciplined, methodical, and dangerous. He's the kind of operative who doesn't get found unless he wants to be—and trust me, he doesn't."

"That right?" Jackson chimed up. "Well, we've handled our fair share of trouble around here."

"I can guarantee nothing like this."

His mannerisms spoke volumes to his distrust of the idea of her inserting herself into their investigation. "How so?"

"Let's just say, he's good at evading, blending in. Knows how to cover his tracks, literally. Men like him are adept at one particular skill ... surviving."

"Great." The deputy let out a low whistle.

"Listen up, folks. This is not a pissing contest!" Tuck's voice was commanding, silencing any further signs of protest. "Hatch has got some experience with this kind of situation, so give her your full cooperation."

The deputies acknowledged her, but Hatch could see the skepticism lurking behind their eyes. Small towns like this didn't usually deal with men like Bishop. That unfamiliarity made them nervous.

Tuck turned back to her. "I had the team ready to head up the west ridge, but something tells me you've got a different plan."

"I followed a broken trail down by the river," she replied. "He crossed to the other side. The tracks went cold over there, but the terrain's dense. If I were him, that's where I'd hide. Thick cover, tough to track."

Tuck stroked his stubbled chin, mulling it over. "Sounds like the right call." He barked orders to his team. "Change of plans. We're starting on the far bank of the river. Let's get moving."

The deputies snapped into action, grabbing rifles, radios, and tactical gear as they filed out of the building. Boots pounded against the pavement as they spread out, voices clipped and urgent over the crackle of radio chatter. Vehicles roared to life, the low hum of engines rising to a steady rumble as headlights pierced the dimming evening.

"Chen, you go with Jackson," Tuck said to his deputy before turning to Hatch. "How about you ride with me?"

Hatch grabbed her go-bag from the back of her SUV and tossed it into Tuck's vehicle, the familiar weight of her gear grounding her as she climbed into the passenger seat.

Tuck handed her a radio. "Signal's iffy up in the mountains, so keep this on you. In case we get split up."

Hatch clipped the radio to her jacket and settled in as Tuck started the engine. The SUV rumbled to life, joining the convoy heading toward the riverbank. Tuck glanced over at her, curiosity still bubbling beneath the surface.

"The people you work for have certainly got connections. Getting assigned to the senator's security detail and now this. Must mean you're pretty damn good at what you do."

Hatch let the silence stretch for a beat before responding. "I go where they tell me to."

"Modesty." Tuck chuckled, shaking his head. "Good quality. Rare these days."

"There's always someone better out there."

"Let's just hope this guy isn't one of them."

"Time will tell."

Tuck grunted his agreement. "We usually deal with tweakers and bar fights. Small town stuff, you know."

"I do. Born and raised in a town not so different from this one."

"You don't say." Tuck eyed her with a bit more reverence. "Where at?"

"Colorado. Four Corners area, just outside Durango." She took stock of the lawman at the wheel. "You remind me of someone."

"Must've been a hell of a guy."

The laugh that escaped her felt good, a release of the tension she'd kept walled up inside her. "He was—is."

Tuck didn't press, and she offered nothing further. "You were right back there, when you said we're not accustomed to situations like this? This's a whole different beast."

Hatch turned to the darkening trees beyond the window. "The battlefield may change, but the mission stays the same. Find the target. Eliminate the threat."

He pressed on the gas. "Let's just hope we're not too late."

TWENTY

COLD BIT INTO BISHOP'S SKIN. HARSH. UNFORGIVING.

He crouched low beside the smokeless fire pit, its faint glow barely warming his fingers. What was supposed to be a swift in-and-out op had spiraled out of control. Now he was playing survivalist in the New Hampshire mountains, and going to be dodging dogs, deputies, and that ticking clock in his head.

Adapt. Survive. Escape. The mantra repeated in his mind, steady and grounding.

Steam rose from the damp socks he'd placed near the fire. Bishop's eyes never stopped moving, scanning the dark tree line for any sign of movement. Every rustle in the woods was suspect, every shadow a potential threat.

From his tactical vest, he pulled up the encrypted file. The light from his small flashlight cast a harsh glow on the image of Maggie Pierce—local girl, investigative journalist now living in the city. She'd taken her mother's name when she left town. Smart.

Why her? It wasn't his job to know. Loose ends led back to orders, and he followed orders. It was the way he'd always worked. *Execute. Don't question.*

Then it came. A bark, sharp and unmistakable.

Bloodhound. Bishop's muscles tensed, instincts kicking into overdrive.

With a cold efficiency, he powered down his phone and tucked it back into his vest. His next steps formed swiftly in his mind, recalculating, adapting. As he began packing his gear, the distant baying of the dog pierced the quiet, carried on the rain-heavy wind. It was faint, but unmistakable. The manhunt had begun.

They were coming for him.

Moving with the precision of someone who had survived the world's harshest environments, Bishop extinguished the fire, scattering dirt and stones over the orange embers until they were cold and lifeless. Wrapping the half-eaten trout quickly, he tucked it into his pack—a necessary source of energy for the night ahead. He pulled on his still-damp jacket, the fabric clinging to his skin, and slung his pack over his shoulders, securing it tight for mobility.

The terrain was unforgiving, but that made it his ally. Bishop knew every ridge, every ravine etched into his mind like a map. The dog might be on his trail, but they were chasing someone who knew these woods better than most.

The baying grew louder, more insistent, closing in as Bishop melted into the rocky terrain. His movements were fluid, silent, each step placed with deliberate care to leave no trace. The rain slicked off his jacket and disappeared into the forest's mist-shrouded depths. His breath remained steady, his pulse unflinching, even as the gap between him and his pursuers narrowed.

Without a second thought, he reached into his pack, pulling out his riflescope. It was cold in his hands, the weight familiar, comforting. He brought it to his eye. The 56mm objective lens cut through the mist and rain, offering crystal-clear visibility for up to a thousand meters. These deputies were sloppy, slogging through the brush, easy to pick off if it came to that.

But then, he saw *her.*

The woman with the twisted scar on her arm. She moved like no one else out there—calm, methodical, lethal. She was not like the rest, guiding their way toward him. The way she carried herself told him everything. She was an operator, just like him.

Bishop's pulse quickened. He felt a flicker of respect—an opponent who might know how to play the game.

But there was no time to admire. Time to move.

The wet socks would have to do.

Just then, his foot hit slick moss. The world tilted violently, and gravity took control. He crashed down the steep slope, sliding with jagged rocks ripping at his clothes. His shoulder slammed into a tree trunk, and pain shot through his body. The fall lasted for fifty feet, ending with a brutal, bone-jarring stop against the base of an oak.

The world spun, darkness clawing at the edges of his vision. He fought it off.

That's when he felt it.

A branch. Thick, gnarled, and embedded deep in his thigh. Blood flowed freely, soaking through his pants. Bishop's breathing quickened, but he didn't allow the panic to take over. He'd seen worse. Been through worse.

Reaching for his rucksack, he dragged it closer with one hand while his other pressed against the bleeding wound. His movements were automatic, every step drilled into muscle memory. Unzipping the main compartment, he pulled out the med kit and flipped it open. He stuck a pen light in his mouth. The familiar tools glinting under the red glow.

First priority, he needed to remove the tree branch imbedded in his thigh. It resisted. Taking a two-handed grip, he yanked it free. In the stillness as fresh pain shot up his leg, white-hot and searing. He gritted his teeth, a low growl escaping as he used the trauma shears to cut away the blood-soaked fabric of his pants.

The laceration was deep but clean—no visible tendon or artery damage, no bone fragments jutting through the flesh. *Could've been worse*, he thought grimly, though the steady flow of blood told him he didn't have much time.

He worked fast, cleaning the wound with isopropyl alcohol, the sharp sting slicing through the cold numbness spreading along his leg.

His breath hissed through clenched teeth, but he didn't stop. *Keep it clean. Infection's the enemy now.*

Next: QuikClot. He tore open the packet, the powder sinking into the gash as he pressed gauze over it. Blood soaked through almost instantly, but he layered more, focusing on control rather than perfection. Finally, the compression bandage. He wrapped it tightly around the wound, firm enough to slow the bleeding without cutting off circulation.

When it was done, he leaned back for a moment, his hands trembling from exertion and pain. The bandage was holding, for now, but this wasn't a permanent fix. *I need proper stitching, or this'll be a problem.* He shoved the med kit back into the rucksack, securing it tightly before glancing around. The clock was ticking, and staying here wasn't an option.

Bishop wiped his brow. Speckles of rain were still falling. It wasn't perfect, but it would keep him moving. He forced himself to stand on the muddy slope. Sharp pain radiated through his body, and he fought the urge not to growl. He had lost blood, too much for comfort, but not enough to stop him. Not yet.

He berated himself. *Sloppy. Amateur.* This wasn't how it was supposed to go. One misstep, and now he was limping through the forest, an easy target for the bloodhound on his trail.

There would be no clean escape now, but he had to keep moving. Distance was his only hope. Find cover. Stay ahead.

As he limped through the dense forest, each step sent fresh waves of pain through his body, but he kept his focus sharp. He'd outsmarted hunters before, and he could do it again.

They were in *his* world now. But the woman, the operator with the scar, would be relentless. Just like him.

But Bishop wasn't done playing yet. This wasn't checkmate.

Moves always had countermoves. And he was about to make his.

TWENTY-ONE

As they reached the riverbank, Tuck killed the engine, and the team stepped out into the damp night air. The sound of the rushing river filled the silence, and the sky above them had faded into deep shades of purple and blue.

Rain drummed the canopy, relentless and uneven, like nature's own arrhythmic heartbeat. Hatch's boots sank into the mud with each step, the wet ground squelching beneath her. Rufus the bloodhound zigzagged ahead, nose to the ground, his enthusiasm wavering with each fading trace of scent.

Beside her, Sheriff Tuck trudged along, water dripping steadily from the brim of his hat. "Don't sweat it," he said, tracing her gaze to the dog and noticing the furrow in her brow. "Rufus always delivers. Found an eight-year-old girl once, five miles out. She'd been missing for three days in weather just like this."

Hatch nodded and fixed her eyes on the forest ahead, her expression neutral. *A dog's only as good as its handler. And Deputy Jackson seems solid enough.* The story about the missing girl stuck in her head, but she wasn't one to put stock in anecdotes—not when lives were on the line. *Still, I've seen stranger things work out in worse situations.*

The incline steepened, trees thickened, and the ground turned slick with mud, each step more precarious than the last.

Rufus froze, tail stiff, nose twitching.

"He's got something." Jackson tightened his grip on the leash. "Fresh scent."

The team moved more quickly, each with their weapons drawn and held at the low ready. Wet leaves made the footing slick. The steady patter of rain against their jackets blended with their measured breathing, visible in the cool night air.

They crested the hill. Jackson held up a fist, halting the trail of lawmen in their tracks. All eyes silently scanned the surrounding area.

Nothing.

No tents. No gear. Just the remnants of a camp hastily abandoned.

But Rufus wasn't finished. The dog's nose twitched furiously as he tugged Jackson toward a patch of disturbed earth in the center of the clearing. Hatch followed close behind. The faint outline of boot prints scuffed the wet ground, barely visible in the mud.

She crouched down, brushing her gloved fingers over the dirt. The surface was cool and damp from the rain, but underneath it was warm.

"Smokeless pit," she murmured, running her fingers through the ash. She brought them closer to her nose, inhaling. "The fire's out, but not cold. He can't have been gone long. Rain hasn't fully soaked the ash yet."

Her eyes swept the clearing, cataloging the details. A few broken branches lay scattered near the tree line, snapped low—probably from the height of a man pushing through in a hurry. Damp leaves clung to the edges of a shallow trench dug into the earth, likely used to channel water away from the camp.

"Recent," Hatch said again, her tone firmer this time. She stood, glancing at the faint boot prints leading away from the clearing. "He packed light, moved fast. My guess is he left in a hurry. Just enough to stay ahead of us."

Tuck moved alongside her. "How close do you think?"

Hatch stood, her eyes narrowing as she tracked the terrain. The tree line thinned, and just beyond, the land dropped off sharply. A sheer cliff loomed ahead, rain washing down its jagged face.

Rufus barked once, his nose leading straight to the cliff's edge.

Hatch kept her voice low and measured as she said, "He went down."

Tuck frowned, looking from the drop-off back to the path they had climbed. "No way we're all going to make it down that. Not in one piece."

Hatch thought for a moment. Too risky, especially with the dog. "We're going to need to double back. Work ourselves around and try to pick up the track again down there."

"Agreed." Tuck turned to his deputies. "We'll have to circle back, cut across the base of the high ground. Hopefully, we'll pick up his trail again."

Jackson nodded. He gave Rufus an encouraging rub of the scruff of his chin.

Tuck wiped the rain streaming down his face in rivulets. "Let's move. We can't afford to lose him now."

They turned to retrace their steps. The firepit was still warm. Bishop was on the run.

But for how long?

DARKNESS CONSUMED THE FOREST. Rain hammered down in sheets now, turning earth to sludge. Each droplet struck Bishop like a tiny bullet, soaking through his Gore-Tex jacket. He pushed on, jaw clenched against the fiery pain in his leg.

The branch had done its damage. Blood seeped through the hastily applied QuikClot gauze. But the rain ... the rain was both enemy and ally. It chilled him to the bone yet washed away his blood trail. Small mercies.

Bishop took each step carefully. Pain be damned. The dense foliage offered cover, but the sodden ground threatened to betray him with every step. His breath came in ragged bursts, visible in the cold air.

His leg buckled. White-hot agony shot up his spine. Bishop bit down, tasting copper. *Weakness gets you killed. Move now, bleed later.*

The weight of his pack dug into his shoulders. Inside: broken-down

M40A6 sniper rifle. Spare magazines. MREs. Survival gear. *A perfect kit, and it still didn't save the op from falling apart.* Each item was a reminder of how sideways everything had gone.

His hand tightened on the sturdy oak branch, his makeshift crutch. The Leupold Mark 5HD scope, nestled in his jacket pocket, pressed against his ribs. *Precision and clarity, useless now, without time or distance. They're not hunting a sniper anymore—they're hunting a man.*

Think, damn it. What's the plan?

Bishop paused, lungs burning, and leaned against a tree. The forest stretched ahead, an inky void. His eyes adapted to the gloom, scanning constantly. *Always a step behind—until they're not.*

Rain lashed his face, soaking his clothes, but it couldn't drown out the thunder of his pulse. *Regroup. Find shelter. Reassess. Don't give them an angle.*

His body screamed for rest, but his mind wouldn't stop. *You know what happens if you stop. They catch you. Game over.*

Bishop froze, eyes locking onto the edge of the tree line. A flicker lit the misty distance. Town lights. So close, yet so far.

Too exposed. Too dangerous. But no choice. You either reach those lights or die out here.

He crept forward. Low. Silent. Rain-soaked leaves muffled his approach. No movement around him, nor sound except for the relentless downpour and his own labored breathing.

How long had it been? An hour? More? The forest had blurred into a monotonous march of shadows and slick terrain. His leg throbbed with every step, the makeshift crutch digging into his palm until it felt raw. He hadn't seen or heard signs of pursuit, but that didn't mean they weren't close. *They're there. They're always there.*

The climb had been brutal, steep and unforgiving, but it gave him this. From his vantage point atop a wooded rise, the lights of the vet clinic came into view, cutting through the rain like a beacon.

The building materialized in the downpour—small, unassuming, tucked on the edge of the sleeping town. A neon sign buzzed faintly through the mist, promising medical supplies within. Antibiotics. Clean bandages. Painkillers. *Everything I need to keep moving. Everything I need to survive.*

He crouched, peering through the thick branches that partially shielded him. His eyes roamed over the clinic and its surroundings. Only one car in the lot, an older model station wagon. No movement inside. *Quiet. Too quiet. But no cameras on the front door, no visible patrols. A risk, but less of one than staying out here.*

The town below slept, blissfully unaware of the wolf lingering at its doorstep. Bishop's hand brushed the hilt of his KA-BAR knife. Cold steel met clammy skin—a visceral reminder of what he was capable of. *In and out. Clean. No room for mistakes.*

Rain masked his approach as he slipped from the tree line. Each step sent fresh waves of agony through his leg, the ground beneath him swaying slightly with each uneven stride. His vision blurred at the edges, a creeping fog he couldn't afford to acknowledge. Blood loss. Infection. Time was not on his side.

But Bishop had a job to finish.

He paused, leaning against a tree for a brief moment, his head swimming as the pounding rain seemed to amplify the roar in his ears. His grip on the oak branch tightened, knuckles white. *Focus. Breathe.* He forced himself upright.

He'd be damned if a little pain, rain, and dizziness would stop him now.

RAIN HAMMERED against the pavement as Bishop moved in complete silence, each step calculated and deliberate. His eyes, sharp and alert, scanned the vet clinic's windows, taking in every detail. Through the glass, he saw her. The woman inside, on the phone, had her back to him. Distracted.

Sticking to the shadows, he circled the building, careful to avoid the glow of the overhead street lights. The barking of dogs echoed faintly from the kennels at the back, muffled by the rain and thick walls of the clinic. He crouched by the rear entrance, his injured leg sending sharp spikes of pain through his body, but he pushed it down. Focus was everything.

He grabbed his lock pick from the side of the pack. Titanium. Lightweight. Familiar in his hand, an old friend. A few deft twists, and the door gave with a quiet click. He slipped inside, pulling it closed behind him without a sound.

The clinic air was thick with the scent of antiseptic and wet fur. Bishop darted his sharp gaze around the dimly lit space, taking in the exam rooms and kennels as he glided past them. The woman's voice was faint now, coming from the front desk. He tuned it out, focusing instead on his surroundings, each movement bringing him closer to his objective.

The operating room.

He found it quickly, slipping inside and shutting the door softly behind him. The room was sterile, cold, and perfect for what he needed. Against the far wall, a glass-fronted medicine cabinet gleamed under the dim light. Inside were the supplies that could save him. He moved toward it, eyes focusing on the vials and bottles lined neatly inside.

Another lock. Child's play.

His hands moved with the speed of experience. The lock clicked open, and Bishop immediately plucked out what he needed. A vial of lidocaine to numb the pain. Antibiotics to stave off infection. An adrenaline shot to keep him conscious long enough to get the job done. A syringe to make it all work.

But as he stepped back from the cabinet, his vision dimmed. Blood trickled through the gauze, down his thigh. The edges of the room blurred for a moment, darkening as dizziness gripped him. He steadied himself against the cabinet, feeling a cold sweat trickle down his spine.

Damn. Worse than I thought.

His breathing came in short, sharp bursts as he opened the drawer beneath the cabinet, his vision splitting and coming back together. Inside were surgical tools. Scalpel. Forceps. Sutures. He knew them well, had used them in field conditions far worse than this. His hands moved by instinct, laying them out carefully on the metal tray beside the operating table.

But his body wasn't cooperating. The blood loss was catching up to him fast, sapping his strength, his focus, with each passing second. His leg throbbed, the hastily packed wound already soaked through with blood. His only chance was to get on the table and treat himself, but even that seemed like a monumental task now.

With a low growl of frustration, Bishop gritted his teeth and dragged himself toward the operating table. His arms shook with the effort, his muscles weakening under the strain. He reached for the edge of the table, his fingers slipping on the cold steel as the room spun around him.

Stay focused. Fix the leg. Keep moving.

His grip faltered. The tray wobbled. Metal instruments teetered on the edge. Bishop's vision swam again, the edges of his world closing in. He fought to stay upright, but his body had reached its limit.

His knees buckled.

And then, darkness.

TWENTY-TWO

Rain tapped relentlessly against the clinic windows, a rhythmic, almost hypnotic sound that only amplified the oppressive silence inside. Evelyn's muscles ached as she wiped down the stainless-steel table for what felt like the hundredth time that night. The clinic, once bustling with activity, was now a hollow shell of itself, filled only with the hum of fluorescents and the occasional soft mewl from the sick tabby in the back.

Her phone, wedged between her ear and shoulder, crackled with Liam's voice, a welcome reminder of home.

"Thanks again for babysitting Chloe tonight, Liam," Evelyn said, exhaustion creeping into her voice. "I know it's been a long day for all of us."

"No problem at all, Ms. Hartwell," Liam replied, his voice warm and reassuring, much like his father's. "Chloe's been keeping me on my toes —she's making sure I don't burn the popcorn for movie night."

"That sounds about right." Evelyn chuckled, picturing her daughter's determined expression. "Everything else going okay?"

"We're doing great," Liam said, his tone lighthearted. In the background, Chloe's voice rang out, unmistakable in its enthusiasm. "Tell Mom I'm staying up 'til she gets home! We've got extra popcorn ready!"

Evelyn's heart softened, the fatigue momentarily lifting. "You two better save some for me."

Liam laughed. "You got it. Just be safe coming home."

"I will." Evelyn glanced at the clock. "I've got a bit of a mess to clean up here. Vet left me with more than I bargained for, and I've got this sick cat to settle in. I'll try to be home before Chloe's bedtime."

"No rush. We've got it covered here."

With a final goodbye, Evelyn hung up, slipping her phone into her pocket. The lightness of the call faded as she surveyed the closed clinic. It always seemed there was one more thing keeping her later, one more task to finish. She rubbed her gritty eyes and headed toward the kennels to check on the sick tabby who lay quietly nestled in its bed.

Just a few more things and she'd be on her way home. She turned toward the supply closet, moving down the hallway —

CRASH.

The sharp sound of metal and glass clattering to the floor rang through the clinic, echoing in the stillness. Evelyn froze, stopped breathing. Her heart leapt into her throat, her pulse thudding loudly in her ears.

Her first instinct was to rationalize it—maybe a shelf had collapsed, or a stray animal had slipped through the back. But something deeper, more instinctual, told her otherwise.

Gripping her phone tightly, Evelyn's thumb hovered over the keypad. She took a breath, shallow and unsteady, as she crept toward the operating room, the source of the noise. The rain pounded harder outside, amplifying the eerie quiet within.

The hallway stretched before her, each step toward the door feeling heavier than the last. When she reached the operating room, Evelyn paused, swallowing hard before gently pushing the door open with a soft creak.

Dim light from the hallway spilled in, casting long shadows across the room. Her eyes scanned the space, darting from corner to corner. Then, she saw it.

A metal tray lay overturned on the floor, glass vials shattered and liquid pooling around them. The room was in disarray, but there was no sign of an animal. No raccoon, no stray cat, nothing that could have knocked the tray over.

Just silence.

Evelyn's breath hitched when she saw it. Him.

RAIN LASHED the forest with relentless force. Each step through the muck was a battle against nature itself, as boots sank into mud, the squelching sound swallowed by the downpour. The air was thick with the smell of damp earth and the sharp tang of ozone. Thunder rumbled overhead, a distant promise of worse to come.

Flashlight beams cut jagged paths through the trees, casting fleeting shadows that twisted in the storm.

"Here!" Tuck's voice barely rose above the hiss of rain.

Hatch moved quickly, her Glock resting steady at her hip, each step deliberate as she knelt beside him. She caught something out of the corner of her eye, a discoloration in the foliage at her feet.

A dark smear stood out against the wet leaves and torn earth.

Blood.

"Beats a damn candy wrapper," Tuck said.

Hatch examined the scene, eyes narrowing. "Looks like he took a bad fall." She pointed to a jagged branch, its tip stained a dark red. "Wound's worse than we thought."

"Maybe he's slowing down?"

"Maybe. If so, that means we might have a better chance of closing the gap."

The hillside had turned into a slick slope of mud and debris. The rain, now a torrential wall of water, cascaded down and turned the forest floor into a treacherous battlefield. Rufus strained against his leash, his nose to the ground, catching faint traces of the fading scent.

Hank walked beside the hound, murmuring soft words of encouragement that were lost in the storm.

"Still on it," he told the others, "but this rain isn't helping. Won't be long before we lose it altogether."

Hatch remained quiet, her focus sharp. The group kept a safe distance from the handler and his K9 partner, giving them room to work. Every so often, Rufus paused, his body tense, then pushed forward again. Time slipped away in the deluge, blurring time and space.

Then Rufus stopped. The bloodhound circled beneath a towering pine, nose twitching but uncertain. His usual confidence faltered, replaced by frustration.

"Scent's gone," Hank called out, shaking his head. Defeat tinged his voice.

The team gathered under the thick canopy, seeking brief shelter from the downpour. The rain drummed overhead, the weight of it seeping into every bone and muscle.

Tuck turned to Hatch, rainwater running in rivulets down his face. "Your call. We're losing light. Losing the trail. Where do you think he's headed?"

She imagined herself in Bishop's shoes—wounded, hunted, desperate for an escape.

"If it were me," she said slowly, "I'd get off the trail. Find cover. Regroup." She scanned the surrounding woods, then her eyes landed on a distant flicker through the trees. The faint glow of the town lights shimmered. "Somewhere with resources."

Tuck tracked her gaze and bobbed his head slowly, rubbing at the salt and pepper stubble dotting his chin. "Makes sense."

Hank knelt beside Rufus, patting the dog's side. The hound seemed eager but weary, his eyes still locked on the fading trail. "Ain't much more we can do tonight," Hank said, the rain dripping from his cap. "Not in this."

Tuck sighed, frustration clear in his voice. "We regroup," he said, decisive now. "We'll catch him before he gets too comfortable."

Hatch adjusted her rain-soaked jacket, exhaustion settling deep into her bones. The storm had sapped their energy, but they'd be back on the hunt soon enough.

Tuck glanced at her, his voice softening. "I'll drop you at your motel. Get some rest, dry off. We'll hit it again in the morning."

"Thanks."

As they made their way back through the soaked woods, the flickering lights of the town remained on the horizon, a reminder that the chase was far from over. The storm would pass, but the hunt would resume. And when it did, Bishop wouldn't have the advantage for long.

TWENTY-THREE

EVELYN'S PULSE HAMMERED AS SHE STEPPED INTO THE DISHEVELED operating room, the sharp beam from her phone cutting through the darkness. The crash of the metal tray still echoed in her ears, but what rooted her in place was the sight before her.

Blood. Dark and viscous. A slick trail leading from the operating table to the far corner of the room.

Then she saw him.

A man slumped against the wall. Clothes soaked from rain and blood, mud caked around his boots. His face, pale and drawn, glistened with sweat. And in his hand, steady despite the agony in his eyes, a gun. And it was pointed directly at her.

Evelyn's breath caught in her throat. Panic gripped her, but her medical instincts kept her feet planted. Fight or flight? Neither seemed possible. The door was too far. His aim? Rock steady.

His voice was a growl, low and ragged. "Don't. Move."

She couldn't have moved even if she wanted to. Her feet were frozen, planted to this spot on the floor. Her eyes flickered over the scene, over him. The jagged tear in his thigh bled steadily, staining the floor. He wasn't a junkie. No, this man had the look of someone who'd seen combat. Someone trained. Military.

"You... you need to leave," she stammered, although the fear made her voice tremble.

A harsh chuckle slipped from his lips. "Tried that." He winced as he shifted his weight. "I need help."

The realization hit her like a gut punch. "You're... you're the one who shot that man." Her voice faltered, the weight of her words heavy in the air.

He didn't confirm it. His eyes remained cold, expression unreadable, but his silence was enough of an answer. She knew what he was capable of—and what that might mean for her.

Evelyn swallowed against her dry throat. The gun didn't waver. She was trapped.

"Okay," she whispered, her hands trembling as she moved toward the medical supplies. "But I need to clean the wound first. If I don't, you'll get an infection."

His jaw clenched, and for a moment, he seemed to weigh her words. Then he growled, "Just. Stitch."

Her fingers fumbled for the needle and thread. The rain outside beat a frantic rhythm on the windows, echoing the fear thrumming through her veins. She worked quickly, her hands steadied by years of experience in the clinic, even though her mind screamed at her to run.

The man watched her, his eyes never leaving her face. As she stitched, Evelyn realized how deep in this mess she was.

Who was he? What was he running from?

"Done," she said quietly, stepping back, the tension in her body refusing to release.

Exhaling slowly, he lowered the gun just a fraction. For a moment, she thought the worst might be over.

But then his legs wavered. He stumbled, catching himself on the edge of the operating table, his eyes still locked on her, but his strength was fading.

"I need ... somewhere to lay low," he rasped, his voice barely more than a whisper. "Just until I get my strength back."

Evelyn's heart sank. He wasn't asking her. He was telling her. Her mind reeled. He wanted to stay? At her house? No. No way.

"You ... you can't stay with me," she blurted, panic rising. "Please ... I can't—"

He shook his head, silencing her plea. "It'll be over soon," he murmured, his voice low, almost soothing. "I'll be out of your hair ... and you'll never see me again."

There was no escape. She had no choice but to comply.

For now.

RAIN HAMMERED AGAINST THE WINDSHIELD, the rhythmic pounding almost drowned out by the roaring silence inside the car. The wipers swiped futilely, barely keeping pace with the torrent as Evelyn gripped the steering wheel so hard her knuckles ached. Her mind spun with frantic thoughts of escape, but every idea ended the same way: badly.

The cold metal of the Sig pressed firmly into her ribs, a constant reminder that she had no way out.

She risked a glance at the man beside her. Bishop sat pale as a corpse, his skin slick with sweat from the blood loss, but those eyes—sharp, calculating, always watching. He'd said little since they left the clinic, but the threat was unspoken but clear.

The porch light flickered through the rain as they pulled into the driveway. Evelyn's stomach twisted with dread. Chloe was waiting inside, oblivious to the danger barreling toward her.

The hum of the engine was muted by the downpour. The car idled in the driveway, filled only with the sound of the rain's relentless assault on the roof. The muzzle of Bishop's gun nudged her side. "Move," he growled, his voice roughened by pain.

No choice. No escape.

The cold rain bit into her skin as she stepped out of the car, every instinct screaming at her to run, to grab Chloe and bolt, but the gun at her back ensured otherwise.

The porch creaked loudly beneath her weight, each groan of the wood like a shot fired into the quiet night. Evelyn reached for the door-knob just as it swung open.

"Mom!" Chloe's eyes darted from her mom's face to the shadowy figure stepping into view behind her.

Evelyn's heart broke as she saw the realization dawning in her daughter's wide eyes.

"Inside," Bishop ordered quietly, his voice as cold as the rain that continued to fall around them. The gun was now hidden from view, but its presence was palpable.

The warm air inside the house felt stifling compared to the chill outside. Liam, who had been sitting on the couch, shot to his feet, his eyes narrowing at the stranger following them inside.

"Who the hell—"

"No." Evelyn's voice was barely a whisper, but it was enough to stop Liam in his tracks. "Don't."

Liam's fists were clenched at his sides. She shook her head slightly, a silent plea not to make this worse.

"I wouldn't," Bishop said flatly, his tone devoid of any warmth. "I'm not here for trouble. Just need a place to let my wound set. Then I'll be out of your way by dawn."

Chloe clung to Evelyn's arm, small fingers digging into her sleeve. Evelyn pulled her closer, her heart pounding in her chest. Bishop scanned the room with a soldier's eye, calculating and tactical, making sure no one made a move that would change the balance of power he held.

"My husband's clothes are in the closet," Evelyn said quietly. "They might fit."

Bishop cast a look to Chloe for a moment before turning back to Evelyn. "Get them. No funny business," he warned, voice low and dangerous.

Evelyn moved to her bedroom closet, her hands trembling as she pulled out a pair of jeans and a flannel shirt. The scent of her late husband's cologne still lingered faintly on the fabric, but she had no time to mourn, not with a gunman in her living room.

She made her way back and handed him the clothes.

"Tie yourselves up," Bishop instructed, directing them toward a pile of scarves draped over a chair. "Don't want any surprises while I change."

Evelyn's hands shook as she followed his command. Liam helped tie the scarves around their wrists, leaving them loose enough to slip out later if the opportunity arose. Bishop wouldn't notice, not with the pain clouding his judgment.

He dressed quickly, but the new outfit did nothing to lessen the danger radiating off him. Sinking into Evelyn's husband's old leather chair, the gun still resting on his lap, his hand never strayed far from it.

"When's your husband coming back?" he asked, his eyes never leaving Evelyn's face.

Her throat tightened as the words caught in her chest. "He won't. He passed away. A year ago."

Bishop offered no sympathy or acknowledgment of her loss. He simply sat there, his back against the leather chair, the weight of exhaustion and pain pulling at his features. But his eyes—the cold, watchful eyes—remained wide open, sharp as ever.

"I just need to rest for a while," he muttered, his voice thick with fatigue. "By morning, I'll be gone. Out of your life. You'll never see me again."

Bishop's hand rested lazily on the gun in his lap. Evelyn knew that until the sun rose, they were prisoners in their own home. And morning couldn't come soon enough.

TWENTY-FOUR

DAWN UNFOLDED IN MUTED GRAYS, THE AFTERMATH OF THE STORM painting the world in damp, tired hues. Hatch's feet pounded against gravel, each step a deliberate rhythm to shake off the night's frustration. Her sharp eyes swept the landscape at the mountain's edge, searching for any sign, any hint of what she might've missed. But there was nothing. Just the soaked earth, and the secrets it swallowed.

Back at the motel, the air was stale. Her clothes, still damp from the night before, hung in the bathroom, dripping in time with her steady breath. Hatch stepped into the shower, letting the scalding water carve away the tension knotting her muscles. Her mind, though, stayed sharp.

The phone buzzed from the counter. She wiped the steam from the mirror with a towel and answered, barely glancing at the screen.

"Tracy," she said, her voice crisp.

Tracy's tone crackled with impatience. "What've you got?"

Hatch leaned against the wall, eyes narrowing at the fogged mirror. "Blood trail. Looks like Bishop's injured. There was a steep drop-off—he's hurting, but mobile. The rain killed Rufus's nose, but Tuck and I are picking up the hunt again this morning."

"Blood's better than breadcrumbs."

"Only if it leads somewhere useful."

The silence on the other end stretched a little too long. Her instincts flared. "Tracy?"

His voice lowered. "We've got more on Bishop."

The faintest click echoed through the line. Banyan, joining the call.

"Line secure?" Tracy asked.

"Now it is," Banyan confirmed, voice calm and measured.

Hatch's grip on the towel tightened. "Since when do we worry about that?"

"Since always." Tracy's voice dipped lower. "Just not always from our own."

"Alright, give it to me straight," Hatch said. "What did you find?"

"Bishop isn't your average hired gun. He's been doing high-level wetwork for Talon for a while. The kind of guy they call when high-value targets need to disappear, both stateside and abroad. He's taken out some big fish."

Hatch's jaw set. "How big?"

"Remember Uzbekistan's defense secretary? The one who supposedly dropped dead from a 'heart attack' during peace talks last year?"

She remembered the news coverage. "That was Bishop?"

"Yeah," Banyan said. "Official story was natural causes, but unofficially? The guy was stonewalling a billion-dollar arms deal. Too many powerful people wanted him out of the way. It needed to be done in such a way as to avert a major upheaval. That's where Bishop came in. One shot, no witnesses, no traces. The autopsy didn't raise a single red flag."

Hatch narrowed her eyes. "And they just... buried it?"

"Buried it so deep you'd need a backhoe to find it. That's Bishop's specialty. He makes the impossible hits look like accidents or acts of God. The bigger the target, the cleaner his work. He's the guy they bring in when subtle isn't an option but deniability still is."

Hatch ran a hand through her hair. "So, in short, he's no slouch."

"Understatement of the year. This isn't some rogue operator we're chasing. Bishop's not just a trigger man—he's an asset. And he's been untouchable for a reason."

"And now he's in the wind working for the highest bidder?"

"That's the catch," Tracy said, voice just above a whisper. "Banyan's been digging. Looks like he might not be as off the books as we thought."

"You're telling me this is a Talon sanctioned operation?"

"Looks that way, but we still haven't been able to confirm for certain."

"There's something else," Banyan said. "Looks like you were right about Sawyer being the target."

"How do you figure?"

"Still firing blanks as to why. When we figure it out, you'll be the first to know." Banyan paused. "We don't know who gave the order, but it wasn't from outside. This one's in the shadows. Deep."

A knot twisted in Hatch's gut. "So I'm chasing a ghost on a mission they didn't want us to know about."

"Exactly," Tracy said. "And you're the one tasked with burying it."

"What's the play, then?" she asked.

"Keep hunting," Tracy said. "We'll keep peeling back the layers here."

"There's one more thing," Banyan said. "You asked me to see what I could dig up on the name Maggie."

Hatch straightened. "And?"

"Looks like the best guess is Maggie Trent," Banyan said. "She goes by Maggie Pierce now. Local girl who moved out of town. She's a reporter. I sent her details to your phone."

"You think Sawyer was a whistleblower? Or blackmailing the senator?" Hatch asked.

"That's the million-dollar question," Banyan replied. "Find her, and we might figure out the bigger picture here."

A familiar rumble broke through the conversation—Tuck's SUV pulling up outside the motel, headlights cutting through the mist.

"Tuck's here," Hatch said, her focus shifting to the task ahead.

"Watch your six," Tracy warned.

"It's my best skill."

HATCH SLID into the passenger seat of Sheriff Roy Tuck's brown SUV, the distinctive Pinewoods logo emblazoned on the side door catching a fleeting glint of early morning light. The interior smelled like fresh coffee, cutting through the faint scent of leather and worn upholstery. She closed the door with a soft thud and glanced over at Tuck, who was already offering her a cup from a local diner.

"Grabbed us both a coffee on the way," he said, his voice gruff but friendly, the warmth of the cup passing into Hatch's chilled fingers.

"Appreciate it," she murmured, taking a sip. The strong, bitter taste hit the back of her throat, jolting her awake a bit more. "How long have you been up?"

Tuck shrugged, pulling his seatbelt across his chest. "Been checking all morning. No reports, no sightings. Not a single thing."

"I went back to the trail. Came up empty too." She took another swig of coffee, the warmth slowly thawing her from the inside out. "He's good, I'll give him that."

"That he is." Tuck scanned the quiet street as he reversed out of the motel parking lot. "But we'll find him. No one just disappears."

There was a shared silence, both of them acknowledging the weight of the task ahead. Hatch was about to press Tuck, see if he had any leads on Maggie—if he was holding back something useful—when the police radio crackled to life.

"Dispatch to Sheriff Tuck, come in."

Tuck clicked the radio on, his brow furrowing. "Tuck here. Go ahead."

"Vet clinic's reporting a break-in. Dr. Hensley's on-site. Blood and broken glass. Deputy Harris en route."

Hatch straightened in her seat, eyes narrowing. "Blood?"

Tuck shot her a glance, a resigned sigh escaping him. "Sounds like it."

Hatch tapped her fingers against her thigh. "Could be unrelated. A hell of a coincidence, though."

"Yeah, well"—Tuck gripped the wheel tighter—"I'm not much for coincidences these days."

"The vet clinic," she said, her voice steady despite the churn of her thoughts. "It's a logical move if he's injured. Supplies. Shelter. But if he's been there, he has either moved fast or left a trail."

Tuck nodded, his eyes locked on the road. "We'll know soon enough."

As they neared the clinic, the small building came into view. Its normally serene facade was marred by shattered glass strewn across the pavement. Tuck slowed down, parking just behind another patrol car. The siren cut off and lights flashed silently, casting a faint red glow on the walls of the clinic.

Tuck killed the engine, and Hatch's eyes swept over the scene, taking in every detail.

TUCK WASTED NO TIME, his voice a calm demand for answers. "What've we got?"

The deputy beside a rattled Dr. Hensley straightened. "Blood inside, but nothing seems to be missing. No signs of forced entry anywhere. Doesn't make sense."

"Doc, when'd you close up last night?"

Hensley fidgeted, tugging at the collar of his white coat, his voice strained. "I didn't. Evelyn Hartwell handled it. My mother had a fall. I had to leave."

Tuck's face tightened. "Have you been able to reach Ms. Hartwell?"

A quick shake of the head, eyes dark with concern. "No. Straight to voicemail. That's not like her."

Hatch and Tuck exchanged a sharp look. They turned and sprinted back to the Tahoe, the air around them crackling with urgency.

Hatch swung into the passenger seat, buckling in as Tuck started the engine. "How far's her place?"

Tuck gripped the wheel, his jaw clenched. "Ten, maybe fifteen minutes. It's outside of town, isolated. Like most places around here."

"Perfect spot to hole up," Hatch muttered.

Her mind churned, ticking through the possibilities. *If Bishop's injured, he'd need time to patch himself up. An isolated house would give him cover, and if Hartwell's there ...* The thought trailed off, replaced by a more unsettling possibility. *She might've walked in on him. Or worse, he could've already been waiting.*

Life had taught Hatch many lessons. One resonated now. *Desperation makes people unpredictable.* It also made them careless. Maybe something to capitalize on. The scenarios kept stacking up, each one darker than the last. Worst case: Bishop's holed up at Hartwell's place, using her as leverage. Or bait.

Hatch's hand brushed the grip of her Glock. She ran through tactical responses in her head. *Assess the house. Secure the perimeter. Force him out if necessary—but Hartwell complicates things. Civilian in play means this won't be clean.*

The Tahoe roared down the winding road, the pines whipping past.

TWENTY-FIVE

Dawn bled through the worn curtains, casting pale light across Evelyn's living room, turning it into a wash of muted grays. Evelyn sat perched on the couch's edge, every muscle coiled tight. An invisible cloak hung over Chloe and Liam, cast by the man holding a gun.

Chloe was small, fragile, her body curled into the armchair like she was trying to shrink into the cushions. Her wide eyes were locked on Bishop's gun, her breath coming in shallow, uneven bursts. Across the room, Liam sat stiffly in a kitchen chair, his jaw clenched, eyes fixed on the man in front of them.

Bishop. Ex-operator, worn down by time and whatever battle had led him here. His clothes were dry, his leg bandaged, but the wound still bled through the fabric. His eyelids drooped, barely holding on, but the gun in his hand stayed firmly in place. It wasn't pointed at them, but its presence was as heavy as the morning air.

Evelyn's heart thundered in her chest, each beat echoing in her ears. This was her home he'd barged into, her daughter he was threatening. And Bishop, a wounded animal backed into a corner, was a threat she didn't know how to neutralize.

The clock ticked, filling the silence with a steady, unbearable rhythm. Then, Chloe's breath hitched—sharp and panicked.

"Mom ..." Her voice was a fragile whisper, barely audible over the tension in the room.

Chloe's small body trembled, her breath quickening, spiraling out of control. Evelyn knew the signs—Chloe was on the edge of a full-blown panic attack.

"Sweetheart, breathe with me," Evelyn said softly, keeping her voice calm even though her insides were screaming. "Just focus on me."

Before she could move closer, Bishop's voice broke through, low and controlled. "Kid. Look at me."

Evelyn froze. She hadn't expected him to speak, let alone try to help. Her pulse spiked, but Chloe's wide eyes shifted to Bishop, locking onto him like a lifeline.

"In through your nose. Out through your mouth," Bishop instructed, his voice steady, almost hypnotic. "Focus. Just breathe."

Chloe's breaths were still fast, but she tried to follow his lead, her chest heaving as she struggled to regain control. Bishop's calm tone cut through her panic like a knife, guiding her step by step.

"That's it," he said, his eyes never leaving hers. "In ... out ... slower now."

Evelyn watched, stunned, as Chloe's breathing began to even out, her trembling subsiding with each deliberate breath. The panic attack that had threatened to consume her slowly ebbed away, leaving only exhaustion in its wake.

"Better?" Bishop asked, his voice still low.

Chloe sobbed weakly, wiping at the tears on her cheeks. "Thank you," she whispered, her voice so small, it barely registered.

Bishop leaned back in the chair, his eyes drifting closed, the gun slipping to rest loosely in his hand. He was exhausted, teetering on the edge of consciousness.

"I'm not here to hurt you," Bishop muttered, his voice gravelly from fatigue. "I just need to rest ... then I'll be gone."

Evelyn's muscles relaxed, but only a fraction. The fear that had gripped her heart loosened, but it didn't disappear. This man was still dangerous, but he was something more. His actions didn't fit the picture of the man she'd feared.

Bishop kept his eyes closed and his grip on the gun. "I'm not your enemy."

The tension in the room shifted, morphing from raw fear to uncertainty. Liam, still seated near the kitchen, broke the silence with a hard edge in his voice.

"Then why the hell are you still holding that gun?"

Bishop's jaw tightened, his eyes flicking open to meet Liam's glare. "Can't afford to take any chances. Not yet."

Evelyn found her voice, trembling with every word. "Chances with who?"

Bishop's eyes drifted to the window, his expression clouded. "I don't even know yet," he said, his voice softer, as if the answer was still out of his reach.

The room fell into an uneasy silence, the air thick with questions no one was ready to ask. Chloe couldn't take her eyes off the man with the gun, her fear dulled by something new—curiosity.

Then, the sound of tires on gravel shattered the stillness. It was faint, distant, but it sent a jolt through the room. Bishop's eyes snapped to attention, his body going rigid. His hand tightened around the gun, knuckles white against the grip.

Evelyn's heart jumped into her throat.

He turned toward Evelyn, suspicion flashing in his eyes. The calm he'd shown moments before evaporated. "Who's coming?"

TWENTY-SIX

THE MORNING WAS A BRUISED PALETTE OF GRAYS, THE SKY HEAVY WITH clouds that pressed down on the land. Last night's deluge had turned the earth into a sodden mess, mud clinging to the wheels of Tuck's Tahoe as it rolled to a stop. The V8 idled low, a steady rumble that barely cut through the thick quiet of the morning gloom.

From the passenger seat, Hatch surveyed the house. Peaceful, maybe, but the kind that comes before a storm. Her fingers brushed the grip of her Glock. Fifteen in the mag, one in the chamber. Her gut told her that it might not be enough.

Tuck opened his door with a soft creak, the sound swallowed by the damp air. He adjusted his Stetson, eyes locked on the house. "Stay put," he muttered, his tone calm but firm.

Hatch's gaze remained transfixed on the house and the potential threat lurking within. "Watch your six."

He nodded and his boots squelched in the wet ground, deliberate steps through the mud. The Tahoe's engine thrummed behind him as he moved up the gravel path, each crunching footfall echoing in the otherwise silent landscape.

From inside the SUV, Hatch cataloged every angle, every shadow. Her eyes swept across the windows, noting possible exits, entry points, cover. She cracked the window, letting the cool air slip in, carrying the smell of wet pine and earth. Her fingers drummed a quick, steady beat on the armrest, matching the cadence of her heart.

Tuck reached the porch, his movement casual, like a neighbor stopping by for a chat. He paused, throwing a glance back at her. Hatch slumped deeper into the seat.

He rapped on the door once. Hollow. Unanswered.

Tuck knocked again, louder. "Evelyn? It's Roy. Got a minute?"

The only response was the soft drip of water off the eaves, punctuating the silence that stretched around them. Hatch's eyes narrowed, scanning for any flicker of movement. A shift of a curtain. The faintest hint of a shadow. Nothing.

Third knock. Tuck's voice remained calm but carried more weight. "Sheriff's office. Anyone home?"

And then, a faint creak. The kind of noise a house makes when it's not empty. Tuck's posture shifted, shoulders tensing as his head angled toward the sound. Hatch caught the movement, her own muscles coiling tighter, ready to spring.

Tuck stepped back from the door, his eyes finding Hatch's through the windshield. A silent exchange passed between them in an instant. Someone was inside.

Hatch's grip on the Glock tightened, her finger hovering just off the trigger. Not yet. She had to let Tuck play it out, see what they were really dealing with.

Tuck turned back to the door, voice steady and calm. "Evelyn, it's important. I need to talk to you."

The wind stirred the pine trees, whispering secrets through the branches. Water dripped from the roof, ticking away seconds as if counting down to something unseen. Hatch leaned forward, her senses keyed in, her breath slow and controlled. Whatever happened next would set the tone, would dictate the play.

One wrong move, and all hell would break loose.

BISHOP DIDN'T NEED to speak. His sharp nod was enough. He slashed the bindings from Evelyn's wrists, leaving red welts behind. His eyes met hers—a silent warning etched in steel. One wrong move, and this would all go south.

Knuckles rapped on the front door. Once. Twice. "Evelyn? You home?" Tuck's voice was friendly but carried an edge, like he was probing for more than conversation.

Evelyn's legs trembled as she rose, her pulse a wild drumbeat in her chest. Behind her, Bishop melted into the shadows, his Sig Sauer held steady, ready to act if needed.

With a deep breath, Evelyn approached the door. She forced her face into a calm, welcoming state and prayed it looked natural. The last thing she wanted was to expose Roy to the man inside. She could only imagine the fallout. She shuddered at the thought. Her fingers curled around the doorknob, and the door creaked open, revealing Tuck, concern etched on his weathered face.

"Morning, Evelyn," Tuck greeted, his tone warm but his eyes searching. "Everything okay? Meant to stop by yesterday, but didn't get a chance. After the craziness, I was tied up for longer than I would've liked. Thought I'd check in."

"Nice of you to stop by. But not a good time right now." Evelyn's façade wavered. She steadied, reminding herself of what was at stake. "Chloe's not feeling well."

"Sorry to hear that. Need some help?"

Evelyn shook her head, a faint smile crossing her lips. "No. She just needs some rest."

Tuck's frown deepened. His eyes scanned the space behind her, lingering on the shadows. "Happy to run to the pharmacy if you need anything."

"No. We're good," Evelyn replied too quickly. Damn, he was being persistent. She wished he'd been this pressing when it came to asking her on a date. "Thanks. I'll give you a call later."

Tuck nodded but didn't move to leave. "You seem a little off, Evelyn. You'd tell me if something wasn't right, wouldn't you?"

The question hung in the air, heavy with tension. Behind her, Bishop's presence was a silent threat. Her heart pounded so loudly she wondered if Tuck could hear it.

"Nothing's wrong," she said, forcing the words out evenly. "Chloe's just got a bug. I was up with her all night. Tired is all."

Tuck's eyes lingered on hers, studying her, searching for any cracks in her story. He opened his mouth as if to press further, but then stopped.

Evelyn's hands tightened on the door, gripping it as though it were the only thing tethering her to the moment.

Finally, Tuck sighed, stepping back. His easy demeanor had hardened just slightly, but he wasn't ready to push. "If you're sure ... I'll head out. But if you need anything—anything—you don't hesitate to call. You hear?"

The tension coiled tighter in her chest. "Thanks, Roy. I appreciate it."

For a moment, Tuck's eyes stayed locked on hers, as if he were reading between the lines of her words. But then he gave her a barely perceptible wink before turning to leave. "You take care of yourself."

The door closed with a soft click, and Evelyn held her breath. She waited, listening to the sound of his boots crunching on gravel, the low rumble of Tuck's engine starting, and finally, the retreating hum of his SUV pulling away.

Her breath escaped in a shaky exhale. She turned, her body trembling with adrenaline, to find Bishop standing by the window, his jaw clenched and his eyes hard as they tracked the sheriff's car leaving the driveway.

"Too close," he muttered, his voice tight with frustration.

Evelyn's hands still shook, her body thrumming with the aftershock of fear. "I got rid of him," she shot back, her voice sharper than she intended. "You don't get to tell me how to handle my friends. I kept you hidden, didn't I?"

Bishop's eyes flicked toward her, something unreadable flashing across his face. For a moment, it looked like he might have said something more, but he turned back to the window, his grip on the curtain loosening but not dropping. The tension in his posture remained, wound tight.

"I'll leave soon," he muttered, more to himself than to her. "Should've been gone by now."

The sheriff's visit had clearly rattled him. Evelyn could sense the delay had made him more dangerous, more unpredictable. He was on edge, and now she really had to tread carefully.

The house fell into an uneasy silence. The sun had fully risen, but its light did little to lift the oppressive atmosphere weighing on her. Bishop might have promised to leave by daybreak, but now his plans had been derailed, and he was still here. And they were still his hostages.

TWENTY-SEVEN

TUCK SLUMPED INTO THE TAHOE, SLAMMING THE DOOR BEHIND HIM LIKE a final verdict. His hands gripped the wheel, knuckles white with tension. The heavy exhale that followed didn't do much to release the pressure building in his chest.

Hatch narrowed her eyes. She recognized that kind of tension—she'd seen it on men right before they broke or pulled the trigger. It was the edge, the line between control and chaos.

Her voice was low, steady, when she asked, "You good?"

Tuck's eyes stayed locked on the house, its silhouette barely visible through the thick morning mist. "My son's in there."

Hatch's pulse quickened. "Why would your son be there?"

"I asked him to make sure the Evelyn and Chloe made it home safely after the shooting. He wasn't home last night when I got back. Not out of the ordinary for him to meet up with some of his friends. Usually leaves a note or a text message," Tuck muttered, rubbing his temple. "I was too damn tired, crashed out on the couch when I got in. But without a doubt, that's his Jeep parked on the backside of the house."

Hatch's mind shifted gears, calculating. The dynamics had changed. This wasn't just a sheriff trying to manage a hostage situation. He was a father with something to lose. Personal stakes like that could lead to bad decisions, dangerous moves.

The Tahoe rolled down the drive. Hatch kept scanning, eyes flicking over the tree line, cataloging potential threats. The wet ground from the overnight rain kept the air thick, heavy. Everything was on the verge of breaking.

"What's the plan?" she asked, her voice cutting through the tense silence.

Tuck clenched his jaw, clearly wrestling with options. "I'm working on it."

Hatch didn't have time for half-measures. "Drop me off," she said, glancing at him. "I'll circle back on foot. Get the lay of the land. Maybe find a way inside."

Tuck whipped his gaze toward her. "Hell no. Not a chance."

"You know it's necessary." Hatch's voice stayed level, but the urgency was undeniable. "Clock's ticking for everyone in that house. Including your son."

Tuck's frustration flared, but Hatch leaned in, lowering her tone. "Remember when we talked about our Army days? This is my wheelhouse. This is why I'm here. You have to trust me."

Tuck's eyes flicked to the scar that stretched across her right arm—a battlefield souvenir, proof that Hatch didn't talk lightly about handling tough situations. He hesitated, despite the reluctance in every line of his face. "Fine. But no hero crap. You get in, you get out. I don't want to be dragging you out of there."

Hatch's eyes locked onto his. "Deal."

Tuck guided the Tahoe into a pull-off, the engine idling as it sat hidden in the shadow of the pines. He reached for the radio. "Calling in backup. Hopefully get the State boys involved, but we can't wait on 'em."

Hatch's hand gripped the door handle, ready to slip out. But just as she was about to move, a pair of headlights cut through the mist. Two black SUVs barreled down the drive toward the Hartwell residence, tires chewing up gravel, engines roaring.

Her gut twisted. "Friends of yours?"

"No." Tuck's face darkened. His answer was low, but it hit like a punch. "And that's a problem."

THE AIR BUZZED WITH TENSION, a charged undercurrent that mirrored the brewing storm outside. Evelyn stood by the window, her gaze fixed on the black SUVs rolling up her driveway. In the distance, a low rumble of thunder echoed. A tempest edged closer.

The lead vehicle's door opened, and Beauregard Covington stepped out, immaculate in his white suit, a jarring, almost grotesque contrast to the rugged Hartwell property. A flash of lightning illuminated the scene, casting stark shadows across the yard and briefly etching his sharp, predatory features against the darkening sky. His calculating eyes swept the scene, devoid of warmth.

Evelyn's pulse hammered in her chest. The storm wasn't the only force closing in. Beside her, Bishop lay motionless on the couch, his breathing shallow but steady, the faint sound barely audible over the growing patter of rain against the roof.

Outside, the wind picked up, tugging at the loose branches of the pines lining the property. The sky flickered again, followed by another low growl of thunder, closer this time. Evelyn clenched her fists, grounding herself in the small, familiar space of her home, though nothing about this moment felt safe.

"Six men," Bishop muttered, his voice low. "Two by the cars, four with him. Armed."

Evelyn fixed her eyes on Covington as he adjusted his cuffs, a deliberate show of control. "He's been circling the reservoir like a shark. My place is the last bit of land he hasn't swallowed."

Bishop's eyes narrowed. "Doesn't look like the kind of man who's used to hearing 'no.'"

"He's not."

Covington took a step forward, dusting off his pristine jacket before raking a hand through his slicked-back hair. His voice rang out, smooth as silk and dripping with condescension.

"Evelyn!" Covington called, the Southern drawl dripping from his tongue like honey over poison. "This little game of yours? It's gettin' old. I've got better things to do than haggle over this … quaint property of yours. A tee time at Augusta, for one, and I'd bet even their bunkers look more refined than your backyard."

Evelyn clenched her fists, nails biting into her palms. Her gaze flicked to Bishop, who hadn't moved. His body was tense, coiled like a spring. He mouthed, make him leave.

Covington's tone darkened, the faux charm vanishing. "You're a stubborn one, just like Malcolm Trent was. And we both know how that story ended, don't we?"

Evelyn's stomach churned, the mention of Malcolm hitting her like a punch to… the gut. Her voice broke, trembling but defiant. She spoke through the closed door. "What did you do to Malcolm?"

Covington's eyes gleamed, stepping closer to the door as he casually adjusted his cuffs. " Poor man just couldn't see the big picture. Tried to stand in my way, and well … sometimes people take a fall when they refuse to see reason. Maybe he should've come up for air instead of drowning in that well of his stubbornness."

The words hit Evelyn like a bucket of ice water. Malcolm's fate had been no accident, and now Covington was standing here, making veiled threats like it was another business transaction.

Bishop's grip on his gun tightened, but he didn't move.

Covington's smirk widened as two of his men flanked him, hands resting lazily on their holstered guns. "Now, why don't we make this simple, Evelyn? Invite me in, and we'll have ourselves a little chat. You know this holdout is pointless. You sign over the deed, and all this goes away. Easy as that. Otherwise …" He trailed off.

Evelyn's heart raced, her eyes flicking to her daughter's room. The air felt heavy, suffocating, but she couldn't give in. She wouldn't.

Her voice shook but held firm. "I'm not signing anything, Covington."

For a moment, Covington's polished facade cracked, a flicker of rage flashing in his eyes before he composed himself. He stepped closer, his voice dropping to a dangerous whisper. "Who've you got in there with you, Evelyn? Someone helping you make these poor decisions?"

Evelyn didn't flinch, but her heart pounded in her throat. Covington scanned the drawn curtains, suspicion blooming in his expression. His men shifted, their hands inching toward their weapons.

Before Covington could push further, a deafening crack split the sky. Lightning struck the old oak by the driveway, splitting the massive tree in two. A branch, thick and heavy, crashed down near the porch, sending a shower of sparks and debris into the air as it combusted into flames.

For a moment, the world froze. Covington's men stared at the flaming tree limb, eyes wide.

The fire licked hungrily at the damp ground, smoke curling into the air. Rain-soaked grass slowed the fire's spread, but the danger was palpable.

Covington barely blinked, his expression dark and menacing. "Proof," he said, voice as cold as the storm overhead, "that accidents happen. Think on that before our next little chat."

With a final, unsettling glance, Covington turned on his heel, his men scrambling to follow. Engines roared to life, the SUVs disappearing around the bend in the driveway.

Evelyn stood rooted in place, torn between the departing threat and the one in her living room. The sky cracked open. A blinding flash of lightning split the air, followed instantly by a deafening clap of thunder that rattled the windows. The strike hit close, too close.

Her gaze snapped toward the edge of the property where smoke curled into the damp morning air. Flames licked hungrily at the base of a tall pine, the surrounding brush igniting in a cascade of hissing and crackling. The acrid scent of burning wood filled her nose.

"Fire!" She stumbled back a step. She flung open the door, the heat of the blaze already radiating through the rain-cooled air.

THE SKY CHURNED, a roiling mass of angry clouds, promising more than just rain. Hatch moved toward the Hartwell house. Tucking tight to the base of a tree, she was able to see into the home through a side window. In the slight gap of the window covering, Hatch spotted a young girl and a teenage boy. Both were bound and gagged in the living room. No sign of Bishop, but the restraints confirmed his presence. He was in there. Somewhere.

Recon shifted to tactical. She tightened her grip on the Glock. A sudden crack of lightning split the sky, illuminating the world brighter for a mere second. A deafening boom of thunder shook the ground beneath her feet. Hatch dropped low.

A massive oak outside the front of the house splintered, its limb crashing near the porch, sending sparks and flames dancing across the wet ground. Despite the rain from the night before, a fire ignited, spreading quickly through the dry debris.

The man standing in front of the Hartwell home didn't notice Hatch tucked in the thicket nearby. "Proof that accidents can happen," The man in the white suit called back. " Think on that before our next little chat." Without waiting for a response, he disappeared into the lead SUV, engines revving as the vehicles peeled away.

Hatch's pulse quickened. Time to move.

Tuck drove the Tahoe up the driveway. As Hatch emerged from the wood line, Tuck sprang from the vehicle. He raised the rear door of the vehicle and appeared a split second later with a shovel. He ran straight for the fire, flinging wet mud onto the flames with desperate force. The rain had bought some time, but the fire still spread, creeping dangerously close to the house.

Hatch didn't hesitate. The fire was a definite concern. But so was Bishop. "I'll be back!" she called to Tuck as she sped past him, moving in a fast crouch toward the house. The closest point of entry was the front door.

She sprinted up the porch past Evelyn. "Stay down," Hatch commanded in a low whisper before kicking the half-opened door wide.

She entered the small, single-story ranch, leading with her gun.

Hatch followed the front sight as she sliced the pie, clearing the fatal funnel of the doorway. The two bound youths looked up in fear. Hatch focused on the potential threat as she stepped deeper inside.

She continued to track the sides of the room, visually clearing as much as possible. Silence. Except for the distant crackling of the fire and the soft whimpers emanating from the young girl. Hatch pushed past the image of the child who reminded her so much of her niece, Daphne.

The living room was clear. No sign of Bishop.

Hatch moved to a narrow hallway. She slowed her pace as she worked her way forward. The bedroom door on her left was ajar. She paused only for moment before shouldering her way inside. It was small. A child's room. Clear.

The last room before the back door was closed. Hatch pressed herself to the wall. She carefully checked the knob. It was unlocked. She steadied herself.

Clearing rooms was a task best done in tandem with others. With Tuck busy with controlling the fire, she was left to go it alone. She counted down. Three, two, ...

Hatch entered with the speed, surprise, and violence of action she'd developed over fifteen years of experience. Lightning flashed through the window at the back of the room, illuminating the interior. Clear.

She exited. Hatch opened the back door and scanned the thick woods, extending up the mountain behind the house. Bishop was gone.

Hatch wanted to continue her pursuit but knew better. He had the high ground. The tactical advantage would be his, and she didn't plan on giving him the opportunity to capitalize on it.

She returned to the living room. Tucking her gun into her waistband, Hatch moved swiftly to help Evelyn free Chloe and Liam from their restraints.

Evelyn's tears mixed with the rain streaming down her face as she swallowed Chloe in a tight embrace.

Tuck appeared in the doorway. His cheeks were smudged in ash. "Fire's contained."

"He's gone." Hatch gestured toward the back of the house. "At least everyone's safe."

Tuck made a beeline for his son. He pulled the teenager close. No words, just an unspoken relief passing between them, before the sheriff locked eyes with Hatch.

"He's wounded. It'll slow him down." Hatch's voice growled. "Which means we can gain some ground."

"We best get to it then."

TWENTY-EIGHT

COVINGTON'S MANICURED FINGERS PRESSED AGAINST THE CREASE IN HIS pantlegs, his irritation simmering just beneath the surface. His driver pushed the Cadillac Escalade's powerful engine along the winding roads. In the rearview mirror, the Hartwell property faded, shrinking into the misty horizon along with the veneer of charm he'd used moments earlier.

His eyes darted to the digital clock on the dashboard. 10:47 AM. Ambrose would be expecting an update.

As the tires met the smooth asphalt, Covington reached for his phone. He tapped the contact list and called the number at the top of it, the CEO of Crystal Springs, Jason Ambrose.

"I've been waiting for an update." The voice on the other end was cold, clinical. No room for pleasantries. "And you know how much I hate to wait."

"Sir, things have been complicated here," he said, tone carefully measured. "I just left the Hartwell property. She's still ... uncooperative."

A sharp pause followed. Covington imagined Ambrose, sitting behind a desk of polished oak, surrounded by his yes men and the myriad lucrative projects in the works. His frustration with the stubborn landowner's defiance was a mark on an otherwise unblemished record. Ambrose didn't tolerate failure. And Convington could tell his boss's patience was wearing thin.

"She hasn't signed?" Ambrose's voice was pure ice. "This should've been settled already, Beauregard. I assumed this call, delayed as it was, would be to notify me that things in that town had fallen in line."

Covington forced the frustration down. "There were … unforeseen complications."

"Unforeseen?" Ambrose's tone dripped with disdain. "Explain."

"The sheriff showed up." He bent the truth and avoided going into the details. Vague was better. It afforded some wiggle room. And right now, he needed as much as he could get. "I wasn't able to reach an understanding."

"And this sheriff, is he going to be a problem?"

"No. I don't think he's aware."

"Good. Things in that town are complicated enough with the Masterson situation. I don't need your incompetence with this matter, adding fuel to the fire." A heavy silence followed.

"I'll take care of it."

"I expect nothing less. Do whatever it takes to make sure she gets the message. This deal is non-negotiable."

"The Hartwell woman will sign." Covington mustered his confidence. "And if they continue to resist … accidents happen. House fires. Brake failures. You know how it goes."

"Talk is cheap. See that it does. This project's momentum can't be halted, not for anyone—especially not for a woman in some backwoods town. Our investors are paying close attention. I lose, you lose."

Covington released the pressure in his chest in a long, slow exhale. "And the other matter—has the leak been taken care of?"

"Being handled as we speak," Ambrose replied. "Focus on your end, Beauregard. You're already behind schedule, and my patience with you is at its end."

The call ended abruptly, the disconnect like the slamming of a coffin lid.

Covington exhaled and tossed the phone aside. His eyes returned to the road as the Escalade devoured the mountain highway. Hartwell was a minor obstacle, a speed bump on his path to power. But Ambrose was right—this deal was too important, and failure wasn't an option.

Small towns had their share of tragedies, and the Hartwell woman was testing fate. Tomorrow would be her last day to reconsider. Or it would be her last day, period.

THE FOREST HELD ITS BREATH, post-storm stillness wrapping everything in a thick, suffocating silence. Bishop moved through the underbrush, each step a battle against the searing pain in his leg. His M65 field jacket, torn and slick with blood, snagged on a branch. He froze, every instinct on high alert. Listening. Waiting.

Nothing but the whisper of his own ragged breathing.

Warm blood trickled down his calf, a stark reminder of his misstep. The torn stitches were a problem. Again. "Just another day in paradise," Bishop muttered, his dry humor a flimsy shield against the pain. Stopping wasn't an option. He gritted his teeth and soldiered on.

The ridge materialized through the mist, and Bishop swept the landscape. Below, the Hartwell house emerged like a grainy image in a developing photograph. Thin smoke still curled from the ground, remnants of the fire barely visible. The county cruiser sat at the porch, its flashing blue lights painting the damp earth in an eerie, pulsing glow.

Two figures stood out clearly.

One—the sheriff—was still battling the fire's aftermath, mud-soaked and wielding a shovel with a desperation that bordered on madness. His movements were sharp and aggressive, as if he could beat back not just the flames but everything threatening his world.

Then the other. Her.

Bishop instinctively brushed his sidearm. The polymer grip was a cold comfort against his palm. She was good. If she planned to catch him, she'd need to do better.

The tables had turned. The predator was now the prey. He had seen operators like her before. Methodical, calculating, unstoppable once they locked on. And she had locked onto him.

His leg throbbed, a dull, insistent pulse that matched the flow of blood seeping through the makeshift bandage. He leaned heavily against a nearby tree, his vision swimming for a moment. The blood loss was worse than he'd thought, and the weight of fatigue pressed down hard. Time was running out.

She disappeared into the house. Tick tock. She'd find his trail soon—the blood, the signs of his escape. The clock was ticking before the chase would start up again.

Time to move.

Bishop pushed off the tree, nearly collapsing as a wave of vertigo hit. His body screamed at him to stop, to rest, but he forced himself forward. Just a light jog through paradise, he thought. Nothing like a morning constitutional with a side of imminent death. The high ground was his best shot, but each step felt like trudging through quicksand. He needed an advantage, any advantage, to keep her off his trail long enough to regroup.

One last glance down the ridge. The fire was little more than a smoldering memory now, wisps of smoke swirling into the morning mist. She was gone from view. Inside, clearing the house. The chase was about to begin.

Bishop's leg buckled as he reached the steeper incline. Agony shot through his body, but he pushed through, his mind snapping into survival mode. When every muscle screamed for relief, you learned to ignore the pain. You learned to keep moving, because stopping wasn't an option.

The forest thickened around him, the mist growing denser. He welcomed the cover, but it slowed him down further. His vision blurred again, black creeping at the edges. He was on borrowed time.

Up ahead, a rocky outcrop jutted from the ridge, offering just enough shelter to give him a moment's reprieve. He collapsed against the cold granite, breath ragged. His hands worked quickly, peeling back the blood-soaked dressing. The wound was angry, deep, and the torn stitches didn't help. Blood still oozed from the gash, but he worked through the pain, packing it with whatever materials he had left.

The pain was blinding, white-hot, but Bishop had endured worse.

He tied off the bandage with trembling hands, each movement deliberate. It wasn't enough to fix the problem, but it would buy him some time.

His sat phone buzzed. Bishop wiped a blood-stained hand on his pants and mashed in the pin code. The scratched screen flickered to life. A single message blinked.

Status on second target?

He typed a quick reply, the words blurring before his eyes.

In progress.

He shoved it back into his pack. Bishop closed his eyes for a moment, the exhaustion threatening to pull him under. No. Not now. The second target could wait. Right now, survival was the only mission that mattered.

He hauled himself upright, his muscles screaming in protest. Each step was a battle—lift, plant, drag, repeat. His combat boots squelched in the mud, each sound a potential beacon to his pursuer. He couldn't afford to leave a blood trail for her to follow. He needed to find better cover, a place where he could regroup without leading her right to him.

The air hung thick and damp around him, the mist coiling its gray fingers between the trees. The rich scent of wet earth and decaying leaves filled his nostrils, mingling with the metallic tang of his own blood. Bishop scanned the terrain, mapping the forest in his mind. These woods were familiar enough, but she knew them too—well enough to track him. She had the skillset, the training. And she was close.

Too close.

That thought spurred him forward, his pace quickening despite the searing pain. He couldn't stop. Not yet. Not while she was still hunting.

Because the moment he stopped, she'd be there.

And then? Game over.

TWENTY-NINE

THE FOREST AHEAD WAS LINED WITH A DARK WALL OF PINE AND OAK. Maggie's eyes flicked to the rearview mirror of her battered Honda Civic, heart hammering against her ribs. This wasn't paranoia. They were watching her now, had been ever since Sawyer's death. The scarred man's face—cold, detached—had seared into her mind that day at Mountain View Diner. His calculating eyes had watched her. Now he was back, waiting for her to make a mistake.

The Civic's engine hummed softly as she navigated the back roads toward Pinewood Falls. She passed the rusted "Welcome to Pinewood Falls - Population 2,187" sign, its faded paint a testament to the town's slow decline. The familiar countryside, once comforting, now felt like a closing trap.

The acrid smell of old coffee and stale fast food wrappers filled the car—evidence of days spent hiding in the woods, sleeping in the car, plagued by fear. But now, there was no avoiding it. She needed her laptop. The small SanDisk Extreme PRO thumb drive Sawyer had given her, tucked safely in her bra, held answers. But without her laptop, those answers were locked away.

"I'm sorry, Dad," she whispered, her voice cracking. The memory of her father, Malcolm Trent, stabbed at her like a knife. His weathered hands, the smell of his Old Spice aftershave, the sound of his laughter—all gone now. His death, framed as an accident, had been anything but. Crystal Springs had killed him. They'd come after her next.

As Main Street came into view, its handful of shops looking eerily quiet in the early morning light, her anxiety spiked. This had to be quick. Keep her head down, grab what she needed, and disappear. Mountain View Diner appeared on her left, its neon 'OPEN' sign flickering, the 'E' permanently dark. Her stomach clenched. The last time she'd met Sawyer here, his voice had been filled with fear and urgency as he warned her about Crystal Springs. Now, he was dead too, and the diner was just a painful memory.

Swallowing her grief, she parked behind the building, killing the engine. The familiar clatter of dishes and smell of coffee drifted from the back door, along with snippets of conversation.

"Did you hear about old man Trent's girl?" a gravelly voice asked. "Heard she's mixed up in some trouble."

Maggie froze, straining to hear more, but the voices faded as the back door swung shut. There was no time for eavesdropping, only survival. She pulled her hood low, stepped out of the car, and made her way toward the apartment.

Her father's teasing echoed in her head. "You're prettier than you know, Mags. Don't hide it." His words had always carried a warmth she hadn't appreciated enough. But now, the baggy clothes and baseball cap had a purpose—keeping her invisible.

The apartment, just two blocks away above Pinewood Suds & Duds, was her first stop. The place where the smell of fabric softener had once been comforting now felt like a trap. As she turned the corner onto Elm Street, her blood ran cold.

The scarred man.

He leaned against a sleek black Dodge Charger parked across the street, a newspaper in hand, pretending to blend in. But Maggie knew better. His eyes scanned the area, lingering on the entrance to her building. The scar running from his eye to his jaw twitched as he assessed the street.

Panic shot through her. She ducked into the shadow of the old oak tree in front of the Pinewood Public Library, her breath coming in shallow gasps. Why hadn't she noticed him sooner? He was watching, waiting for her to walk through the front door. If he saw her, it was over.

She needed another way in.

She put together an escape plan. The door at the back of the laundromat connected to the stairwell to her apartment. Hopefully, she could sneak in without him seeing.

Heart pounding, she circled the block, sticking to the shadows as she reached the alley behind Pinewood Suds & Duds. The hum of washing machines greeted her as she pushed open the back door. Every creak of the stairs sent chills down her spine. One wrong move, and he'd know she was there.

At the landing, she paused, seeing the broken dresser outside her apartment—a reminder of her last hurried escape. Another lifetime ago.

As she stepped inside, her heart sank. The apartment had been torn apart. Drawers yanked open, clothes strewn everywhere. They had been here, searching. For the thumb drive? She rifled under a pile of unfolded laundry on her bed to where her laptop should have been.

Gone.

"Damn it," she muttered, her chest tightening with frustration. They had beaten her to it. Desperation surged. She grabbed a duffel bag from under the bed, stuffing it with clothes. The laptop was gone, but she still had the thumb drive. That had to count for something.

She left her apartment and was about to head back down the stairwell when the door leading to the street creaked open.

Him.

Her heart leaped into her throat. He was here, and she had seconds—maybe less—before he found her. Her eyes darted to the broken dresser. Without hesitation, she shoved it toward the top of the stairs. The heavy wood caught the edge of the wall and careened down just as the scarred man rounded the corner.

The crash was deafening, the loud noise reverberating through the stairwell.

The dresser slammed into him, pinning him against the banister. He cursed, a string of expletives echoing through the stairwell. "You can't run forever, Maggie!" he snarled, his voice a mix of pain and fury.

But Maggie didn't wait. She bolted down the back stairs, heart racing, breath rapid. She burst through the laundromat, startling an elderly woman folding her sheets.

"Sorry, Mrs. Grayson!" Maggie called out, not breaking stride as she dashed for the back door and sprinted to her car.

Her hands shook as she fumbled with her keys, trying once, then twice to get her car door open. The engine roared to life just as the scarred man reappeared, sprinting toward her.

"Stop right there!" he shouted, his hand reaching inside his jacket as he closed the distance between them.

Maggie floored it. The Civic's tires squealed as she peeled out on the wet pavement. The scarred man slapped the side of the car, the impact jolting through her as she swerved onto Main Street.

In the rearview mirror, she watched him shrink into the distance, standing in the middle of the street, frustration painted across his scarred face. He pulled out a phone, no doubt calling for backup.

Maggie gripped the steering wheel, her knuckles white. They'll find me again. But not before I expose them. Not before I bring them down.

The memory of her father flooded her mind, his scent lingering as if he were there. She had to finish what he'd started. The "Now Leaving Pinewood Falls" sign flashing by, and she knew she was running out of time—and options.

I'll be back to finish this, Dad. I promise.

THIRTY

HATCH MOVED THROUGH THE DENSE WOODS, HER STEPS MEASURED AND quiet, unlike the questions swirling in her mind. The early morning sun barely penetrated the thick canopy overhead, casting dappled shadows on the wet ground. The forest smelled of damp earth and pine, the remnants of last night's rain clinging to the leaves. She could feel herself closing in on Bishop. The fresh blood smeared on the foliage confirmed it.

Tuck had remained back at the Hartwell house, tending to the family. She knew she would be faster without him, but the added value of having another gun on her side wasn't lost on her.

Her phone vibrated softly in her pocket. Without slowing, she pulled it out and saw the incoming call was from Tracy. She tucked behind a moss covered tree and answered.

"Got an update on Bishop." She continued to can her surroundings for any sign of movement. "I'm in pursuit. His trail is fresh—he's wounded."

"Good." Tracy was tense. "Once you locate him, do not engage."

"I thought I was tasked with bringing him in."

"Orders have changed. Containment is your primary objective now. Don't let him get away."

"And then what?"

"The General is sending a team to handle it."

Hatch frowned, suspicion crawling up her spine. "Handle it? What does that mean?"

"It means how it sounds."

"You're telling me that Thorne is sending a hit squad to take out Bishop?"

"You're not one for mincing words." Tracy let out a frustrated sigh. "Look, I don't like this anymore than you. But Bishop's a threat. The powers that be feel he's too dangerous."

Hatch let the thought marinate. "Is this what my future holds? A couple ops get a little dicey and Talon sends in a clean-up crew?"

"Not gonna happen. Not on my watch."

"What happens when you're not watching?"

"No time for this train of thought."

A long silence stretched across the line. Then Tracy spoke again, this time his voice flat. "Remember, not my call. This tasking is coming from the top."

Her jaw tightened. "And I'm supposed to report directly to Thorne now?" She couldn't mask the disdain in her voice.

Before Tracy could respond, a familiar voice cut through the static, calm but laced with an edge. "Listen, Hatch," Banyan said. "Something about this stinks. Watch your six. Trust your instincts. This runs deeper than even we know."

The line went dead, leaving Hatch in the eerie stillness of the forest. She shoved the phone back in her pocket.

She pushed deeper into the woods, her senses on high alert. The air was cool and damp, with the lingering trace of rain-soaked decay. Hatch slowed as she reached a section of disturbed ground, the leaves overturned, and the dirt scuffed in a way that set her on edge. She knelt, her sharp eyes scanning the pattern of the tracks. Bishop's, no doubt.

Her fingers traced the edge of a print, noting its depth. The left boot's indentation in the muddy surface was deeper. He's favoring his right leg. Hatch's eyes followed the uneven spacing of the prints, the shortened gait confirming her suspicion. The injury's catching up with him.

She straightened, her grip tightening on her weapon as she scanned the dense woods ahead. *Wounded doesn't mean harmless. A cornered predator is the most dangerous kind.*

Her muscles tensed as she rose, her eyes flicking through the trees, listening for any sound that might betray his position. Every fiber of her being was tuned to the forest, the stillness pressing down on her like a physical weight.

Then, in the quiet, she heard it. A twig snapped off to her left.

In one fluid motion, Hatch spun toward the sound, her Glock raised, finger hovering near the trigger. Her eyes locked on the front sight, every instinct screaming for her to act. Her breath slowed, and time stretched out, her entire focus zeroed in on the movement behind the trees.

A deer stared back at her. Its large brown eyes blinked, innocent and unaware, as it stood frozen in place, watching her.

Hatch let out a slow breath, lowering her weapon as the tension in her muscles relaxed, but the unease remained. The deer lingered for a moment longer, then darted off into the underbrush, disappearing into the shadows as quickly as it had appeared.

Her pulse pounded in her ears, but she forced herself to refocus. The ground around her was disturbed. Bishop had definitely come this way. She crouched again, looking at the blood-streaked dirt.

The air was thinner as she ascended the ridge, her breath steadying with the climb. She slowed, her senses on high alert. Something was wrong. The forest was too quiet now, too still. The faintest shift of the wind sent a prickle down the back of her neck.

Then, a faint rustle came from behind her, the sound of leaves shifting against the damp forest floor. It was too deliberate to be the wind, too quiet for anything large. Her breath hitched, and she spun around, her eyes cutting through the dim light.

No deer stared back at her, no animal darted into the underbrush. Just the empty woods, silent except for the faint patter of water dripping from the trees. It was then that she spotted the source.

Bishop materialized from behind a dense network of shrubs. He now stood just a few feet away, his Sig Sauer trained on her chest. His face was pale, his leg gushing blood, his breathing labored, but his eyes were sharp. No doubt about it, this man was a killer.

"You've been following me," Bishop rasped, his voice hoarse. "Who sent you?"

Hatch's gun wasn't on target. He definitely had the advantage. She slowly canted the front site upward. "How about you lower that thing before I put a bullet in your head?"

"Not my first rodeo. I don't plan on dying today."

"Might be out of your hands."

The thin mountain air and the invisible line in the dirt were all that separated them from life and death.

HATCH WASN'T able to bring her pistol to her eyeline. But the micro adjustments she'd made coupled with the years of range time gave her confidence that she had a shot. Her eyes remained locked on Bishop's. His on hers. The gun in his hands shook ever so slightly. Time passed slowly during this tense standoff in the middle of the forest. They stood only a few yards apart, each holding the other's life in their hands.

"Lower your weapon," Hatch said.

"You first."

They both knew that wasn't happening. A moment of silence stretched between them, broken only by the soft rustle of the trees and their own controlled breathing. Neither of them moved.

"Let's not kid ourselves," Hatch muttered, her index finger taking the slack out of the trigger, stopping at the breakpoint. Her task was to contain him. Wait for the cavalry. The current circumstance was making it incredibly difficult to follow orders. "You fire, I fire. No way I miss."

"I don't miss," Bishop replied. "Ever."

Hatch's eyes narrowed, calculating. "Then it looks like we're at an impasse."

Bishop didn't falter. "Seems that way."

Hatch searched for an opening, but Bishop wasn't going to give her one. He was wounded, sure, but still dangerous. They both teetered on a razor's edge, and a single wrong move would send them tumbling into a lethal exchange of gunfire.

"If we're both about to die," Bishop said slowly, "we might as well lay our cards on the table."

"Only one of us is about to die." But time bought opportunity. Facing off against someone of Bishop's caliber meant that every opportunity counted. "Start talking."

"For starters, how about you tell me who sent you?"

Hatch thought about lying. There'd be no point to it. Her only advantage was the truth. Anything else was a gamble. "Talon."

"Go figure." A bitter laugh escaped Bishop's lips. "Did they tell you why? Or are you just another one of their lap dogs?"

"Definitely no one's lap dog." Hatch didn't like the thought. "They told me you were once an asset. That you decided to market your skills to the highest bidder."

"So that's the spin." His head gave an almost imperceptible shake. "The stories they tell. And you believe them?"

"No reason not to."

"Really?" He paused long enough to consider his next words. "Let me run another story by you. Then you can tell me which one smells like the truth."

"I'm all ears." Hatch made another slight adjustment to her point of aim.

"What if I told you that I hadn't gone into business for myself? What if I told you this was a sanctioned hit?"

"You're saying this was a Talon op?"

"Don't look so shocked." His gun hand trembled. His face grew paler. "When money's at stake, the moral compass has a tendency to shift. And when big money's on the table, that shift is seismic."

Hatch thought about the intel Tracy and Banyan had shared. The high-value target eliminations. She also analyzed Bishop's non-verbal tells. Something she'd learned in her years of interrogation. The body spoke louder than words. And everything about Bishop told her that he was telling the truth. Now she was left with the hard decision of accepting it. If she did, where would that leave them?

"Talon doesn't authorize executions." She felt the words coming across as hollow, but she needed to buy more time to process.

"They're the puppet masters. Pulling strings, moving pieces, treating us like disposable assets. Use us until our knowledge becomes a threat."

"You're saying that's what happened here? You complete a hit and immediately become expendable?"

"Did it ever dawn on you that your being here might be part of the equation?"

"You're saying I'm a pawn in all this?"

"Don't look so shocked. But if you really think on it, you'll see."

Hatch replayed the original tasking, the change in orders, the slow piecemeal of information she'd been doled out. All of it originating from one man.

"I can see you're puzzling it out in your head," he said. "You know I'm telling the truth."

"Who ordered the hit?"

"Came from high."

Hatch's stomach twisted as the name left her lips. "Thorne?"

"Bingo. And now you've been tasked with bringing me in. See how it all fits?" He seemed pleased with himself. "They put you in place. Must've known you'd come after me. Slowly manipulating the chessboard, even going so far as to attach you to the local law enforcement. Makes for an easy cleanup."

"But why all the trouble? You've pulled off hits in the past."

"You have no idea what's at play here, do you?" Bishop tightened the grip on his weapon. "Thorne's in bed with Crystal Springs. Has been for years. Buying up land, selling it off, raking in millions while destroying lives."

"Okay. Doesn't explain why you targeted Sawyer. Assuming you didn't miss."

"Like I said, I don't miss," he said coolly. "Sawyer was the target. He had the proof. He was about to blow the whistle—land deals, wire transfers, all of it."

"So they sent you to kill him? Why do it in such a dramatic fashion? Why not make it look like a car accident or something like what you did in Uzbekistan? "

"Ah, so you are familiar with my work?" A slight crack in his otherwise stoic façade cracked. "The senator was losing traction in the polls. The powers that be decided nothing boosts a politician's ratings more than an assassination attempt. He's a shoe in for the next term. And that means Crystal Springs can continue to scoop up the water rights. And the money continues to flow."

"Why send me? Seems like they planned for everything."

"They did. Every good conspiracy needs a patsy." He shrugged. "Guess it was my turn. No easier story to sell. I'm sure that they would've created a money trail, showing that I'd been paid by some environmental extremist group looking to settle the score. Whatever they come up with, I'm sure the public will buy it. They always do."

Hatch thought about the ease with which Talon had erased or manipulated the fallout from her operations. Nothing Bishop said rang false. In fact, everything he said made sense. "If you knew all this, why not just pop smoke and disappear?"

"I wasn't sure until now. Until facing you."

"Okay. But why not get out of town?"

"Because there was a hiccup." Bishop's expression darkened. "Sawyer was talking to a reporter. If that information gets out, it'll bury them."

"You have another target."

"The reporter. A woman by the name of "Maggie Pierce."

The last name on Sawyer's lips was now a target on Bishop's. Dots were connecting.

Hatch clenched her jaw. "You've done this before? Civilian targets?"

"You ask questions you already know the answers to. You've never been given a kill order?"

"Overseas, yes. Even then, it was never a civilian." Hatch knew the dirty business of war all too well. It shouldn't have come as a surprise. "And never from Talon."

"Give it time." He eyed the gun in her hand. "You sure they didn't give you that order...for me?"

"Locate and contain only."

"What do you think they'll tell you to do once they know you've located me?"

She knew a team was inbound. She knew they'd been tasked by Thorne. Hatch could feel the weight of Bishop's words settling in, each revelation a piece of the puzzle clicking into place. Talon, or the very least Thorne, wasn't just involved in covering up dirty deals—they were orchestrating the whole damn thing. And she had been an unknowing partner in all of it. Now that she knew, what Hatch did next would define her.

"What does Maggie have that they want?"

"Sawyer made a handoff. A thumb drive containing the damning evidence," Bishop's voice was growing weaker. The injury slowly draining him. "He apparently gave it to her before I put a bullet in him. Everything's on it, proof of the conspiracy. If it sees the light of day, Crytal Spring's empire crumbles. And with it, anyone who's connected to it."

"That means Thorne," she said, more to herself.

"They want her dead before she can do that."

Hatch's pulse quickened as the reality set in. Talon wasn't just sending her after Bishop, they were sending her to wipe out anyone who could expose their operation. Bishop, Sawyer, Maggie, they were all loose ends, pawns on a board controlled by people who viewed them as expendable. And now Hatch realized she was now added to the list.

Hatch struggled to read the face behind the gun. "Why take you out before the mission's complete?"

"Guess they have other plans. Bet you didn't know that Reeves is a former Talon guy."

Hatch's reaction betrayed her.

"Guess they didn't tell you that." He cocked an eyebrow. "I'm sure if you did some digging, you'd find he actually never left Talon."

It made more sense. His resistance to any of her suggestions. He knew all along. He's the failsafe. "And now they're sending another team in."

Hatch let the information speak truth. "Why me?"

"That's the million-dollar question." He waited for a beat before continuing. "How do you erase the trail?"

"Bury it deep."

"Layers upon layers. I kill Sawyer. New target keeps me on location. Can't disappear. You're tasked with hunting me down. You start getting close. Instead of giving you the green light, they tell you to hold in place and send in a team."

"Tracy would never—"

"Probably right. My guess is that Tracy knows about as much as you." Bishop gave a sigh of resignation. "Kill the killer, then kill the killer's killer."

"And the clean up?"

"C'mon. You've been in the organization long enough to see how easily they can dust off an op. Like we were never there."

"How would you write the ending?"

"Look at us right now. Standing here with our guns pointed at each other. You shoot me, I shoot you. I'm the villain and you're the fallen hero. Either way, all traces are erased."

"And what about Maggie?"

"I'm sure the alternate has already been called into play. Reeves is probably closing in on her as we speak, if he's not already finished her off."

Hatch understood why she'd been sent. The cold truth settled over her. "Thorne is going to erase us both,"

Bishop shrugged. "Welcome to the expendables club."

For a moment, the forest was eerily still, the tension between them palpable. Neither lowered their weapon, but something had shifted. They weren't enemies anymore. Just two people caught in the same web, marked for death by the same people who had once commanded their loyalty.

"So what's the play?" Hatch asked, her mind already running through possible escape routes, alliances forming in real time.

Bishop lowered his gun just slightly, enough to signal the beginning of a fragile truce. "We find Maggie. We protect her. And then we burn Crystal Springs to the ground."

Hatch reluctantly agreed. They were no longer on opposite sides of this fight. The rules had changed, and she wasn't about to play by the old ones anymore.

"Looks like we're in this together," Hatch said.

Bishop's eyes remained sharp despite the weariness etched in his face. "Guess so. But make no mistake. It's survival of the fittest and I'll kill anyone who gets in the way. And this team they're sending will be a Tier One asset."

Hatch lowered her Glock just a fraction. "If we can't outgun them, then we'll have to outwit them."

THIRTY-ONE

THE HANGAR ECHOED WITH THE HUM OF MACHINERY, A CAVERNOUS SPACE of steel and shadows. The sleek, black Range Rover idled near the far corner, its tinted windows concealing the lethal intent within. Under the harsh fluorescent lights, four men moved in tandem, silently covering the ground at a rapid pace. This wasn't a mission of recovery. It was a hunt, and the target was already marked for death.

Stone, the team leader, paced in front of the vehicle, his eyes cold and calculating beneath the scar that traced down his temple. He glanced at his watch, then over to the men prepping for the mission. There was no need for conversation; they knew their roles. Their bodies moved like clockwork, tactical vests tightened, weapons loaded, suppressors screwed into place with soft clicks that echoed like a countdown.

"Gear check. Final," Stone growled, his voice gruff and commanding.

His HK hung across his chest, a silent promise of violence. He stopped by the Range Rover's tech specialist, Mac, who was perched atop the vehicle, attaching the final pieces of satellite equipment to the roof.

"Comms are live," Mac confirmed, his voice clipped. "Green light."

Stone turned to the team. "This is weapons-free. Rules of engagement are simple: Bishop goes down. No negotiations, no captures. Just dead. Clear?"

A silent ripple passed through the squad as they double-checked their gear. These were men of war, and the pre-battle routine electrified them. Suppressed rifles gleamed under the dim lights, magazines clicked into place. Stone's cold eyes swept over them, making sure each man was ready. This wasn't a mission where anyone got a second chance.

Grimm slung his sniper rifle over his shoulder, eyes already scanning the distance as if lining up the kill in his mind. "Ready to roll, LT."

Stone clicked his earpiece, stepping to the side as he made the call. "Command, this is Talon Team. Over."

A crackle of static came through before the calm voice of Thorne responded. "Go ahead, Talon Team."

"We're geared up and rolling out. Requesting an update on Bishop's position." Stone pulled a tablet from his vest. The screen flickered to life, displaying a topographical map of the rugged terrain in the White Mountains, a mix of steep ridges and dense forest—a sniper's playground.

The voice on the other end replied, "Last known location is grid coordinate 44.1260° N, 71.4336° W. Hatch is on his trail, pursuing him up the ridgeline. Expect contact soon."

Stone's jaw tightened as he memorized the coordinates. "Roger that," he muttered, ending the call. The rest of the team stood ready, rifles in hand, eyes sharp and focused.

He glanced at Grimm, who gestured toward the mountains visible in the distance. "Bishop's up there. The longer we wait, the farther he gets."

Mac tapped his tablet. "Satellite feed's up. I've got heat signatures pinging on the ridge—one's definitely Hatch, the other's gotta be Bishop. They're not far."

"Move out," Stone ordered, his voice low but authoritative. "We take him down. No loose ends."

The team climbed into the Range Rover, the vehicle's engine purring like a panther ready to pounce. Grimm slid into the front seat, his rifle resting across his lap, eyes locked on the tree line ahead. Mac sat in the back, his fingers flying over his tablet as he monitored the feed, while Rook adjusted his gear, checking his sidearm with a focused intensity that belied his usual reckless energy.

As the Rover rolled out of the hangar and into the open air, the dense forest lay ahead, the perfect place for a man like Bishop to make his stand. The sun hung low on the horizon, casting long shadows across the road as they drove toward the ridge.

The vehicle slowed as they neared their drop point, tires crunching on gravel. The tension in the air was palpable, each man processing the gravity of the mission in his own way. Grimm's fingers flexed on his rifle, his trigger finger itching for the kill. Rook's leg bounced, clearly eager for the moment when things would explode into chaos. Mac focused on the screen, watching for any sign of movement.

Stone pulled the Rover to a stop just below the ridgeline, the forest around them unnaturally quiet. The team dismounted, moving like shadows through the underbrush, their movements efficient, controlled. The scent of damp earth and pine filled the air, the soft rustle of leaves the only sound as they advanced.

"Got a visual," Stone whispered into his mic. "Two targets. Moving."

THIRTY-TWO

MAGGIE'S HANDS SHOOK AS SHE CLUTCHED THE PHONE, HER KNUCKLES white against the worn plastic. The familiar smell of old upholstery and the faint scent of pine from the faded air freshener dangling from the rearview mirror filled the cramped interior of her Honda Civic. She hadn't been here in years, not since high school, when this pull-off on the edge of the woods was a haven for stolen kisses and whispered promises. Now, it served as a temporary refuge.

She'd been driving around for hours since escaping her apartment, constantly looking over her shoulder, expecting to see the man with scarred face around every corner. The woods surrounding the lot loomed darker than she remembered, the faint rustling of leaves carried by the wind setting her teeth on edge.

Maggie's pulse pounded in her ears as she gripped the phone tighter, her thumb hovering over the screen. *Where do I go now?* She thought, her mind spinning in circles. There was nowhere left to run, and the ticking clock felt like a noose tightening around her neck. *If I call the wrong person, if I trust the wrong hand... it's over.*

The phone was heavy in her hand as she dialed the only number she could think of. Sheriff Tuck picked up on the third ring, his steady voice grounding her in the chaos.

"Tuck."

"Hi Sheriff. It's Maggie."

"If you're calling about your dad, I've got to apologize. I've been caught up in this mess with the senator."

"Then I think you're going to want to hear what I have to say." Her voice trembled when she replied, the fear threading through every word. "Sheriff ... they're after me. I don't have much time."

Tuck paused for a moment and when he spoke again, his voice was calm yet urgent. "Who's after you? What's going on?"

Maggie squeezed her eyes shut, her breath coming in shaky gasps. "It's all connected—the senator, Crystal Springs, everything. They killed Sawyer because of what he knew, and now they're coming for me. I've been running, but I can't hide much longer."

"Slow down, Maggie. Start from the beginning. Who's after you?"

Her heart raced, every beat like a hammer against her ribs. "I don't know ... all I know is that he's got to be working for them."

"If what you say is true, best way I can help is for you to come down to the station. Think you can do that for me?"

"I have proof."

"Listen to me, Maggie." Tuck's voice cut through the static in her head, firm and steady. "You need to come into the station. I can protect you. Bring whatever proof you have, and we'll figure this out.."

She wanted to believe him. Needed to believe him.

"I don't know if I can, Sheriff." Her voice was barely a whisper. "I don't know who to trust anymore."

"You can trust me," Tuck said, his voice slow and calm. "I swear to you, Maggie, no one's going to get to you. Not while I'm around. We'll keep you safe, I promise."

"Okay," she said, her voice steadier now. "I'll meet you at the station. But Sheriff, please be careful. These people will stop at nothing."

"Just get here, and we'll figure it out together."

Maggie hung up, her heart still racing, but the panic no longer threatened to swallow her whole. She had a plan now, and she clung to it like a lifeline. Slipping the phone into her pocket, she pulled the hood low over her face as she pulled out onto the road.

REEVES LEANED against the hood of his black Dodge Charger, the soft patter of rain tapping against the slick metal and pooling in the shallow dents of the pavement. The diner behind him buzzed with muted life, the occasional clatter of dishes filtering through the rain-dampened air. Across the street, the sheriff's station.

He pressed the phone to his ear, his expression flat as the senator's voice crackled through the line, taut with panic. As usual.

"Dammit, Reeves! You told me you had her! You said this was handled!"

Reeves closed his eyes, letting the senator's hysteria wash over him without reaction. His scarred face remained impassive, carved from stone. He'd dealt with men like the senator all his life—powerful, desperate, and weak when the heat turned up. He took a long breath before speaking, keeping his tone calm, almost bored.

"Hey, she slipped my grasp. But it's handled."

The senator's reply was an explosion of words, his voice shrill with fear. "Handled? *Handled?* She's out there, Reeves! If she talks—if she even hints at what she knows—the whole operation is blown wide open! I'm dead! Do you understand that? Dead!"

Reeves smirked to himself. *Pathetic.* The senator, with all his money and power, couldn't keep his nerves in check for more than five minutes. He let the silence stretch before answering, letting the senator stew in his panic.

"Relax," Reeves said, his voice smooth as silk. "I know where she's going."

The senator sputtered on the other end, disbelief dripping from his tone. "How the hell do you know that?"

"Call it a hunch." Reeves didn't mention that he'd tapped the sheriff's station phone lines two days ago when he'd stopped by to brief Tuck on the senator's speaking engagement. It was a redundancy plan he'd put in place so he could stay abreast of any developments. It served him well now. Maggie had no idea the mistake she made when placing that call.

"There's a lot at stake here. You understand that?"

Reeves rolled his eyes, his patience thin. "I'm not an amateur, Senator. She's panicking, which means she's going to run straight into the arms of someone she thinks can protect her."

"And who the hell is that?" the senator snapped, his paranoia bubbling over.

"Sheriff Tuck."

There was a pause on the line, the senator's breathing slowing as the pieces began to click into place. "So, you're going to intercept her?"

Reeves wiped the rain from his scarred face with the sleeve of his jacket. "Don't worry about how I'm going to handle it. Just know that it'll be handled."

"No mistakes this time, Reeves. I can't afford them. Get rid of her. Permanently. No more slip-ups."

"You think I don't know what's at stake?"

"And the sheriff?" The senator's question was cautious, filled with concern. "What if he sticks his nose in too deep?"

"If Tuck tries to play the hero, well … we'll cross that bridge when we come to it."

The senator didn't respond, but Reeves could hear the unease in his silence.

"You hired me because I finish what I start," Reeves continued, his tone flat and final. "And I don't leave loose ends."

The senator exhaled shakily. "Just make sure it's clean. I don't want any of this getting back to me."

"Consider it done," Reeves said, the promise hanging in the air like a death sentence.

Ending the call without waiting for a reply, he slipped the phone into his jacket pocket as he surveyed the deserted street.

Maggie was running on borrowed time, and she didn't even know it. She thought she had a chance, thought she could run to Sheriff Tuck and find safety. But all she was doing was leading him straight to her.

There would be no more mistakes. No more close calls. Maggie Pierce was about to walk into a trap, and Reeves would be there to greet her.

With a bullet.

THIRTY-THREE

Sheriff Roy Tuck stepped through the front door of the station, the worn soles of his boots scuffing against the tiled floor as he made his way inside. The familiar scent of old coffee and lemon cleaner greeted him but did little to mask the mud and smoke clinging to his uniform. He ran a hand through his disheveled hair, shaking off the morning's chaos, but the weight of the day clung to him like the grime on his clothes.

Behind the front desk, Pearl, his longtime receptionist, glanced up from her paperwork. Her silver hair was pulled back in a neat bun, and her reading glasses were perched low on her nose as she peered over the top of them, her quiet charm instantly putting Tuck at ease. Pearl had been at the station longer than anyone could remember.

"Good morning, Sheriff," Pearl said, her soft Southern drawl wrapping around the words with a warmth that only Pearl could manage. "Rough start?"

Tuck gave a tired chuckle, rubbing the back of his neck as he approached the desk. "You could say that. Dealt with a fire up at the Hartwell place. Got tangled up in more mud than I'd care to admit. And the smell?" He sniffed his sleeve, shaking his head. " I'm guessing you can smell that smoke from there."

Pearl's nose wrinkled delicately, her eyes crinkling at the corners. "Sure can, but I wasn't going to say anything. You've certainly had worse. Grab yourself of cup of coffee. Just brewed a pot." She glanced at the clock on the wall. "Forgot to mention, you've got someone waiting for you in the interview room."

Tuck's tired expression shifted to one of alertness. "Maggie Pierce?"

"No, Sheriff. Someone from the senator's office. They've been here about fifteen minutes now, said they needed to speak with you about the shooting yesterday." Pearl's voice was calm, but Tuck caught the flicker of concern behind her eyes. "Seemed urgent."

"Guess that coffee will have to wait." Tuck's jaw tightened at the mention of the senator's office. Of course, the senator's people were sniffing around already. Yesterday's shooting had been messy—too many moving parts, too many loose ends. And now, with everything else going on, the last thing he needed was some politician's lackey adding to the pressure.

"Thanks, Pearl." Tuck pushed himself off the counter. "Let Maggie know I'll be with her as soon as I'm done here. Might need you to keep an eye out for her, okay?"

"I'll keep a close watch, Sheriff." Pearl's tone was soft but laced with a hint of worry.

Tuck straightened his back, squaring his shoulders as he moved down the hallway toward the interview room.

The room was brightly lit, the harsh overhead lighting casting sharp shadows across the plain walls. At the center of the table sat a man in a tailored suit, polished and pristine, out of place in the small-town station. His briefcase rested beside him, open but orderly, and he didn't bother standing when Tuck entered.

"Sheriff Tuck," the man said smoothly, his voice carrying the practiced politeness of someone used to navigating uncomfortable conversations. "I appreciate you taking the time. I'm here on behalf of Senator Masterson. We need to talk about yesterday's incident. There's been a development."

Tuck nodded and asked, "Can I get you a cup of coffee?"

"No thanks. I've had my fill."

"Alright then." Tuck shut the door behind him, his eyes narrowing slightly as he took a seat across from the man, folding his arms across his chest. "Let's talk."

MAGGIE PULLED into the small gravel parking lot outside the sheriff's station, her hands gripping the steering wheel so tightly her knuckles whitened. Her heart pounded in her chest, and she scanned the area for any sign of the man who had been after her. For the first time in days, there was no immediate threat. But that didn't ease the knot in her stomach.

She took a deep breath, trying to steady her shaking hands before pushing open the car door and stepping out into the brisk morning air. The early sun was still low, casting long shadows over the quiet town. Everything seemed too calm, too ordinary, compared to the chaos she'd been running from.

The small sheriff's station stood ahead, a modest single-story building. It seemed almost too simple a place to offer any kind of protection from the mess she was tangled up in. Maggie hurried inside, her pulse quickening again as she glanced around.

The receptionist behind the front desk was an older woman with kind eyes. Her soft silver curls fell from her bun, framing her face. She looked up as Maggie entered.

Her smile set Maggie at ease just a little bit. "Good morning, dear. You must be Maggie. Sheriff Tuck told me to expect you."

The words caught in Maggie's throat. "Yeah, is he available?"

The receptionist gave an apologetic look. "He's finishing up with someone in the interview room, but he won't be long. Would you like to wait in the back, somewhere more private? I'll make sure he knows you're here."

Maggie hesitated. The adrenaline dump from earlier made her jittery. "Thank you."

The receptionist stood up slowly, the years of working in a small-town sheriff's station evident in the way she moved with deliberate care.

She motioned for Maggie to follow her past the secure door, leading her into the main office.

The station was small—only a few desks scattered throughout, each one neat and organized, unoccupied at this early hour. A police radio crackled softly in the background, its voice barely above a whisper in the otherwise quiet space.

The receptionist gestured to a chair by the wall. "Why don't you sit here, hon? Can I get you some coffee while you wait?"

Maggie lowered herself into the chair, her nerves still frayed. "Coffee sounds good. Thank you."

"How do you take it? Cream? Sugar?"

"Just black," Maggie replied, her voice wavering.

Pearl disappeared toward a small kitchenette, leaving Maggie alone with her thoughts. She pulled the thumb drive from her jacket pocket, her fingers brushing over the small firefly keychain attached to it. Her father had given her the nickname "Firefly" when she was little, and this keychain was one of the few things left of him. It had been her constant companion since she'd fled. As she sat here now, it felt like a lifeline.

Maggie contemplated the risk. The proof was on this drive—everything Sawyer had risked his life to gather, everything her father had fought to protect. But was it enough? Would anyone believe her, or would they come for her before she even had a chance to tell her story?

The receptionist returned with a steaming cup of coffee, her soft voice breaking through Maggie's thoughts. "Here you go, dear," she said, offering the cup. "Careful now, it's hot."

Maggie took the coffee, the warmth of it seeping into her cold fingers. "Thank you."

Pearl gave her a concerned look, her hands resting on the back of the chair opposite Maggie. "You alright, sweetheart? You look a bit shaken."

Maggie managed a weak smile. "Just been a rough couple of days."

The receptionist's eyes softened with understanding. "Sheriff Tuck's a good man. If anyone can help, it's him."

Maggie wasn't sure if even Tuck could stop what was coming. The image of the man who had chased her—his scarred face, the cold calculation in his eyes—was burned into her mind. She had no doubt he'd find her again, and next time, she might not get away.

As she sipped the coffee, the faint murmur of voices drifted from the back office, where Tuck was still in his interview. Maggie glanced at the door, wondering if Tuck had any idea of the bomb she was about to drop on his doorstep. She clenched the thumb drive tighter, the small firefly keychain pressed into her palm.

It wasn't just her life at stake anymore. It was her father's legacy, Sawyer's sacrifice, and everything Crystal Springs was hiding. And now, sitting in the quiet station, she realized she was both out of time, and out of places to run.

THIRTY-FOUR

THE RUMBLE OF THE ENGINE CUT OFF, LEAVING AN EERIE STILLNESS IN THE forest. Hatch's heart thudded in time with the rustling leaves, not by the wind, but by footsteps. She crouched beside Bishop. The damp earth chilled her knees, and the acrid smell of gunpowder still hung in the air, mixing with the sharp tang of Bishop's blood.

"Four-man kill team," Hatch muttered.

"We're exposed," Bishop grimaced through clenched teeth. He glanced toward the ridgeline, muscles tensed, his body ready for an attack. "They'll find us."

Her voice was cold, clinical, a professional assessing the situation. "And if the General sent them to take us both out, you know they're capable."

Her mind ran through every possible scenario, each more hopeless than the last. Outgunned, outnumbered, and Bishop was barely hanging on. Some days, she really hated this job.

"They won't stop until we're both dead," she whispered, her voice barely audible above the soft hum of the forest.

Bishop looked worse than death warmed over, his skin pale, his breaths coming in ragged gasps. He winced, clearly fighting the pain, but the blood loss had drained most of the fight from him. They wouldn't survive a direct encounter. Her options dwindled by the second.

BISHOP GRUNTED, leaning against a tree for support, his breath uneven. "Probably Stone's team," he rasped, eyes flicking around as if expecting shadows to materialize from the woods. "They do Thorne's dirty work. And they're ruthless."

Hatch's pulse quickened, her hand instinctively moving to her Glock. "So what's the play?"

"Not much in the way of options. Or time."

Her fingers brushed against the small case tucked inside her vest. Banyan's creation. Simulated death—an ace up her sleeve, but one she hadn't expected to use so soon. She withdrew the black case slowly, weighing her options.

"Only chance we've got," she said, "is for you to play dead."

Bishop raised an eyebrow, his skepticism palpable. "They won't trust it. They'll check."

Hatch's eyes darkened. "Exactly. And that's why you won't be faking it."

Bishop squinted, eyeing the small black case warily. "What's that?"

Hatch opened the container, revealing the dermal patch inside. "A little gift from Banyan. Simulated death—lowers your heart rate, body temp, everything. They'll think you're dead."

Bishop looked at the patch and then back at Hatch, clearly distrustful. "So you're going to slap that thing on me, and I'm supposed to trust it's not going to turn me into an actual corpse?"

"Not like we've got a lot of choices here. You bleed out, or they put a bullet in both of us. Banyan said it works. No trace, no foul."

Bishop let out a shaky breath, glancing at the patch again, then at the tree line where the kill squad would soon emerge. "Well … here's to Romeo and Juliet," he muttered, voice laced with sarcasm.

Hatch smirked, quickly pulling the patch from the container. "We're not dying today. You just need to trust me."

He hesitated, his breathing labored, his pulse erratic. "Trust is a big ask right now."

"Maybe," Hatch replied, pressing the patch to his neck. "But it's the only card we've got left to play."

Bishop grunted as the patch made contact with his skin. "If this doesn't work—"

"It'll work," Hatch interrupted, but the weight of uncertainty hung in the air between them. The chemical smell briefly filled the space around them as she snapped the vial inside. Bishop's body immediately began to slow, his breaths growing shallow, his eyes fluttering shut.

"Remember," Hatch whispered, wiping the blood from her palm onto his neck to sell the illusion. "Stay still. Let me handle the rest."

Bishop's lips barely moved, his final words a soft murmur. "I better wake up from this."

As his pulse faded, Hatch stood, her muscles tense, posture rigid. She smeared more blood from Bishop's leg onto her own arm, grabbed her knife, and cut across her palm, wincing at the sting. She took fresh blood and wiped it across Bishop's neck and face. It would have to be enough.

The approaching kill team's footsteps grew louder. They were close now—boots crunching through the underbrush, the faint rustle of tactical gear as they advanced. Her pulse quickened, but she kept her exterior calm. She adopted a posture of exhaustion, every muscle tense beneath her mask of weariness.

They were coming.

And Hatch had to sell this, because if she didn't, she and Bishop were both as good as dead.

THE KILL SQUAD moved through the mist, four figures blending seamlessly with the dense underbrush. Silent, deadly, each man a professional operator. Their gear—Crye Precision combat suits, ops-core helmets with night-vision mounts, and HK416s at the ready—

marked them as Talon's elite. Stone commanded the team from the front. These men weren't here to capture. They were here to clean up.

Spreading out, they formed a tight perimeter. Hatch crouched by Bishop's body, her breath steady despite the tension coursing through her. She was outnumbered, her cover story fragile at best.

"Hold it!" Stone's voice cut through the mist, a harsh command. His assault rifle was leveled at her chest, the red dot of the laser sight trained right over her heart. The other three operators moved into position, flanking her with silent precision.

Hatch raised her hands slowly, careful to keep her movements calm, deliberate. Her eyes flicked to the still form of Bishop beside her. "He's down," she said, her voice betraying just the right amount of exhaustion. "Bishop tried to ambush me. I didn't have a choice."

Stone's helmet dipped slightly, his gaze flicking to Bishop's prone form and back to Hatch. Suspicion hung in the air between them, thick and heavy.

"No gunshot," Stone muttered, his voice cold. His rifle remained steady.

Hatch forced a breath, angling the blood-smeared knife in her hand. She held it up just enough for them to see the crimson streaks glistening on the blade. "No time to pull my gun," she said, the frustration in her voice carefully placed. "Had to use the knife. He bled out fast."

Stone took a slow, deliberate step forward, his eyes never leaving hers. "Knives don't make noise," he acknowledged, but his tone carried no belief. He gestured to one of the operators. "Rook. Check him. Verify."

Rook moved without hesitation, his rifle slung low but his body tense, ready. He crouched beside Bishop's body. He slipped off one of his gloves and pressed two fingers against Bishop's neck, searching for a pulse. The forest seemed to close in around them, the silence stretching thin and taut like a wire about to snap.

Hatch's heart pounded in her chest, each beat thudding loudly in her ears. Her entire focus was on keeping her breathing even, her expression tired but resolute. If these guys didn't buy it, they were both dead.

Her fingers flexed at her side, itching toward her Glock, but it wouldn't matter if this went south. There'd be no time to draw.

Rook's hand lingered on Bishop's neck for a beat longer than Hatch would have liked. The other operatives' rifles stayed trained on her, their fingers light on the triggers, ready to react.

Finally, Rook glanced up, his face hidden behind his visor, but his voice clear. "Lights out."

The tension eased, but only slightly. Stone's weapon lowered a fraction, but his body remained taut, like a spring coiled too tight. The other men shifted but didn't fully relax.

The team leader stepped closer. "Name's Stone. Don't think we've had the pleasure." His face mere inches from Hatch's. "You got lucky. Bishop's a dangerous man."

"Luck had nothing to do with it."

Stone stared at her for a long moment. "He's one of the best."

"Was."

"Right." Stone paused and seemed to be choosing his next words wisely. "Guess that's one loose end we don't have to tie."

"What's the other?"

He stepped back, suspicion lingering in the air. "You'll know as soon as I do."

Stone reached for his comms. Hatch gripped the ribbed handle of the knife in her hand. The next few moments would prove whether the theory she and Bishop had hashed out was correct. If they were right, the quiet surrounding them was about to be shattered into a million pieces.

THIRTY-FIVE

THE MOUNTAIN AIR PRESSED IN, DENSE AND SUFFOCATING, AS FOG BEGAN to snake its way between the trees. Every breath felt sharp, every sound magnified by the stillness of the forest. Hatch stood motionless, the weight of her Glock hanging at her side like a lifeline. Her pulse thrummed in her ears, but outwardly she was calm, her every move calculated.

Rook, the squad's pulse-checker, knelt beside Bishop, performing a quick inspection, though Hatch knew he hadn't been thorough. Grateful he'd made that mistake, one she planned to capitalize on. But they weren't stupid, and mistrust simmered beneath the surface. She could almost hear their thoughts: *What's wrong with this picture?*

Hatch remained still, every nerve in her body quivering with the anticipation of what might come next. She calculated the distance between her and the man closest to her. If she made a move, she might be able to disarm him, but the others would gun her down before she got halfway. The odds were bleak. Then again, when weren't they?

A small twitch caught her eye—Bishop's fingers, just the slightest movement. It was barely perceptible, but enough to let her know the patch was working. He was playing his part perfectly, teetering on the line between life and death.

Suspicion swirled behind Stone's calm exterior. He stepped forward, his suppressed HK416 still pointed downward but clearly ready to swing up at a moment's notice. Hatch's pulse quickened, but she kept her expression neutral. The tension in the air was thick, electric.

"What's the cleanup plan?" Hatch asked, her voice breaking the silence, casual but probing. She needed to keep them focused on her words, keep the distrust from fully taking root. "Grizzly attack? Rogue militia? How are you selling this to the locals?"

Stone's eyes narrowed, clearly not interested in banter. He didn't respond, just pulled out his sat phone and stepped slightly to the side, making a quick call. His team stayed alert, their eyes darting between Hatch and Bishop, their fingers twitching near their triggers.

The soft glow of Stone's phone illuminated his face in the mist, a sharp contrast against the gray morning haze. The sound of his conversation was low, but Hatch's ears picked up the words she'd been dreading.

"We've got confirmation," Stone said, his voice steady. "Bishop is down."

There was a brief pause, a heartbeat of silence that stretched into eternity. Then, the cold voice of command cut through the static, sharp and decisive. "And Hatch?"

Stone glanced at her, eyes narrowing further as if weighing something. "She's alive. Took out Bishop before we arrived."

Another long pause. The silence seemed to stretch the seconds into hours, every muscle in Hatch's body coiled tight, ready to spring. Then, the final command came through the line, the words hanging in the air like a death sentence:

"Clean slate."

MAGGIE PERCHED on the edge of the chair, her fingers clenched tight around the firefly keychain. The cold, sterile environment of the police station did nothing to calm the rising dread crawling up her spine from the moment she arrived. The fluorescent lights overhead flickered once, and her eyes darted to the clock on the wall. Each slow, deliberate tick amplified her anxiety, hammering home the fact that time had run out.

Pearl, the kindly dispatcher, had tried to comfort her earlier, offering coffee and making small talk. But the warmth in her tone had felt artificial, and Maggie could sense that Pearl didn't understand the depth of her fear. She appreciated the gesture, but what she needed now was action, not pleasantries. Every second wasted felt like another nail in her coffin.

Her eyes locked on the door of the interview room. Sheriff Tuck had been in there for what seemed like hours, and she was growing increasingly desperate. She needed to tell him, to warn him. If they didn't move fast, everything could fall apart.

Then the door opened. Maggie straightened, her heart thudding in her chest. The soft murmurs behind the door signaled that something serious was unfolding. Sheriff Tuck stepped into view and Maggie felt a sliver of hope. She began to rise from her chair, ready to speak, to beg him for protection.

But the flicker of hope was snuffed out as quickly as it had come.

The door swung open wider, and behind Tuck, another man stepped through. Maggie's breath caught in her throat, her body freezing as if the air had been sucked out of the room. The man with the scar. The sight of him was like a punch to the gut, his gun pressed into Tuck's back. Time slowed and for a moment, all Maggie could see was the man who had haunted her thoughts since their last encounter.

Reeves's presence was an icicle of dread piercing her chest. He was calm—too calm—as he moved forward, the barrel of his pistol pressed against the sheriff's back. His eyes, cold and calculating, flicked toward Maggie, and a smirk tugged at the corner of his lips.

"I don't think you're going anywhere, Sheriff," Reeves said, his voice smooth.

Sheriff Tuck's reaction was immediate, a low growl rumbling from his throat. "What the hell is this?" His hands were raised in slow compliance, but the anger simmering in his voice was palpable. He didn't move, but Maggie could see the tension in his shoulders, the barely restrained fury behind his eyes. Tuck was a man used to control, but Reeves had just tilted the balance in his favor.

Reeves's smirk deepened. His sole focus was on the small object clutched in Maggie's hand. The firefly keychain dangled, and with it, the thumb drive.

"I think you've got something my employer needs," Reeves said, his voice chilling in its quiet confidence.

Maggie's fingers tightened around the drive, her knuckles white. Her body refused to move, fear paralyzing her in place. She wanted to scream, to run, but her legs felt like lead. All she could do was watch, helpless, as the situation spiraled out of control.

Tuck, ever the protector, spoke with as much confidence as one could muster under the circumstances. "You're not getting her. You want to hurt someone? You'll have to go through me first."

Reeves didn't flinch. If anything, he seemed amused by Tuck's bravado. "I don't need to kill you, Sheriff. But I will if you force my hand."

Maggie's heart pounded in her chest. The weight of the moment pressed down on her, the very real possibility that Reeves would kill them both if this went wrong. She had to do something. She had to speak.

"He's lying, Sheriff. Don't let him take me!" Her voice was small, shaky, but desperate.

Tuck didn't take his eyes off Reeves. "That's not going to happen," he said firmly. But Maggie could hear the tension in his voice, the concern he was trying so hard to mask.

The air in the room grew heavier as the standoff intensified. Reeves's patience was wearing thin. "You've got no idea who you're dealing with, Sheriff. The people I work for? They'll burn this town to the ground to get what they want."

The threat hung in the air like a dark cloud, and Maggie's terror grew. She knew Reeves wasn't bluffing. She could feel the weight of his words, the cold reality that there were forces at play far beyond her understanding.

Tuck remained stoic, his mind clearly calculating. But Maggie could see the brief flicker of his eyes toward the gun against his hip, and then to the door. There were deputies outside, but they were out of reach. No help was coming.

"I'm getting impatient. I'd hate for this to end with a bullet in the wrong place." Reeves tilted his head, his smirk never faltering. "Can you live with that? One pull of this trigger, and it's over."

The tension in the room was suffocating. Maggie was frozen in place, her body trembling, pleading with Tuck to do something— anything. The moment stretched unbearably, both sides locked in a dangerous game of chicken.

THIRTY-SIX

HATCH'S STOMACH TURNED, THE KNOT TIGHTENING WITH EVERY BREATH, but she forced herself to stand tall, her face a mask of calm. *Clean slate,* she thought. *No emotion, no fear.* But the truth gnawed at her. They didn't just want her dead. They needed her erased, neutralized. The wind whispered through the pines, carrying with it the smell of damp earth and blood-soaked pine.

Stone pocketed his phone, the weight of finality in the gesture. His expression hardened, the cold gleam in his eyes unyielding. "Sorry, Hatch. Orders are orders. Looks like you got Bishop, but not before he got a shot off. Don't worry—you'll go down a hero."

Hatch smirked, hiding the fear crawling up her spine. "Not much for awards," she said, her voice steady, despite her pulse pounding in her ears. "Definitely not much for dying either. The benefits package is awful."

Stone chuckled, a low, humorless sound, as he raised his HK416. "Nobody ever is."

Time slowed.

Bishop erupted from the ground, a force of raw survival instinct.

Rook, the operator kneeling over him, didn't even have time to scream. Bishop drove a jagged stick into the man's throat with a wet crunch. Blood sprayed across the forest floor, pooling at the man's feet as he gurgled and collapsed. The forest, already deathly still, seemed to hold its breath.

Hatch launched herself into the fray.

Stone spun, bringing his gun up.

Bishop was faster. He snatched the fallen operator's MP7A2, and a burst of automatic fire ripped through the air, forcing Stone to dive behind a boulder. Dirt and pine needles flew up as a chaotic barrage of bullets tore through the space where Stone had been standing.

Bishop pivoted, his movements calculated and precise despite the blood oozing from his own wounds. Crack! Crack! Two quick bursts, and the second operative fell, his blood seeping into the mossy ground.

Hatch turned her aggression toward the man closest to her. Caught in the decision loop, he hesitated, his eyes darting between Bishop's onslaught and Stone. That fraction of indecision cost him. Her KA-BAR flashed, the blade finding the narrow gap between the man's body armor. The grunt of pain was sharp, desperate, as he reached for her, his fingers brushing her jacket as they tumbled toward the edge of a steep drop-off.

They hit the ground hard, pine needles scattering as they rolled, each fighting for the upper hand. Hatch twisted, driving her knee into the man's groin. His grip loosened for just a moment—a moment she seized. She shoved him hard, sending him toppling over the edge. His scream echoed, a fleeting, chilling sound that ended with a sickening crunch as his body hit the rocks below.

Stone reemerged from his cover, firing relentlessly at Bishop. A round struck the limp body Bishop had dragged in front of him as a shield, the heavy armor absorbing the brunt of the impact. But it wouldn't hold for long.

In one fluid motion, Hatch dropped her knife, drew her Glock, and squeezed the trigger. Two shots. Center mass. Stone staggered. The impact to his vest drove him back. A momentary look of disbelief crossed his face before the third and final shot found its mark between the team leader's eyes. Blood plumed into the woods behind him as he dropped to his knees, before crumpling forward, lifeless.

For a moment, the forest was silent. Hatch stood, panting, her Glock still raised, scanning the area for any sign of movement. Her hands trembled, the adrenaline coursing through her veins making it impossible to steady them. But she didn't lower her weapon. Not yet.

Bishop slowly rose, wiping blood from his face with the back of his hand. The final remnants of Banyan's reagent were wearing off. The mask of death he'd worn was replaced by a cocky grin.

Hatch holstered her Glock but kept her hand close. "Not bad for playing dead."

"Not bad for saving my ass," Bishop's smirk widened. "Maybe next time we skip the whole 'fake death' thing. The hangover's a bitch."

Hatch allowed herself a tired chuckle, the tension in her body beginning to ease. "No promises."

She glanced around at the bodies scattered among the trees. Blood stained the forest floor, a testament to the violence they had unleashed. The silence felt wrong. More were coming. They both knew it.

"We need to move," Hatch said, her voice low, eyes scanning the tree line. "No telling if there's more on the way. When they come get here, I'd rather not be around for the family reunion."

THE THUMB DRIVE felt impossibly small in Maggie's trembling hand, the firefly keychain dangling loosely as she stretched it toward Reeves. Her breath came in shallow bursts, heart racing as she stared down the barrel of his gun. The cold metal was fixed on her, steady and unyielding, the threat more real than ever.

Reeves' eyes narrowed, his hand twitching, ready to snatch the drive. "Give it here, Maggie," he hissed, his voice low, each word laced with menace. "Make this easy."

Her throat tightened, her pulse drumming in her ears. The second cup of coffee Pearl had given her was still in her hand, the warmth seeping into her palm and steam curling lazily into the air. Maggie's mind spun, grasping for a way out, but there was none. She was trapped, time slipping away. She needed a distraction, anything.

The crackle of the sheriff's radio cut through the air, snapping the silence as deafening as a gunshot. Maggie flinched, her eyes flicking to the sheriff, who stiffened as the dispatcher's voice came through loud and clear.

"We've received multiple calls from up the mountain. Gunfire reported. Caller says it's coming from over the ridge. Sounded automatic."

The sheriff's jaw tightened. Maggie's breath caught. Over the ridge. It was close to here. Hope flickered, but she buried it deep, unsure of what it meant.

A deputy's voice followed, casual, dismissive. "It is hunting season. Probably some idiot testing his new rifle."

The dispatcher pushed back, her tone sharper. "Caller said it sounded like a war zone."

Reeves shifted, his eyes darting to the radio, just for a second. Maggie saw the opening and took it.

She shot to her feet, thrusting the thumb drive forward, her voice shaking but loud enough to cut through the air. "Here! Take it! Just take the damn thing!"

Reeves lunged, his hand reaching for the drive, his focus locked on her.

That's when Maggie struck.

With one sharp movement, she flung the cup of scalding hot coffee straight into his face. The liquid hit him with a hiss, burning his skin. Reeves recoiled, his scream of pain echoing in the small office. One hand flew to his face, the other tightening on the trigger in reflex.

The gun fired. The sound was deafening, the bullet slamming into the cubicle partition just inches from where Maggie had stood. She dropped to the floor, heart hammering in her chest. That shot had been too close.

Reeves staggered, his face twisted in agony, coffee dripping down his cheeks and neck. The sheriff didn't waste a moment. In a single fluid motion, Tuck drew his gun.

Two shots rang out, the crack of gunfire splitting the air. One of the bullets hit home, striking Reeves in the side. A grunt of pain tore from his throat, his hand clutching at the wound as blood began to stain his shirt. His eyes burned with fury as he raised his gun and fired blindly, forcing the sheriff to dive behind a nearby desk for cover.

Tuck's shouts cut through the chaos. "Maggie, run!"

Bullets tore through the office, shredding papers and wood, the space filling with the harsh sounds of destruction.

Maggie pushed herself up, adrenaline pumping through her veins, and bolted for the back door. Her breath was fast and ragged, her chest burning as she shoved through the exit. The cold air hit her hard, biting at her skin as she burst into the alley behind the station.

Her feet pounded the pavement, legs trembling but refusing to stop. Her heart raced, faster than her steps, as she sprinted toward safety, lungs screaming for air.

Maggie risked a glance over her shoulder and saw him. Blood smeared his side, dripping onto the ground with each step, but the pain didn't slow him down. His face was a mask of rage, the gun still clutched in his hand.

He was coming for her.

THIRTY-SEVEN

THE FAINT SMELL OF GUNPOWDER CLUNG TO THE HIGH PINES. HATCH stood beside Bishop, her breathing steady, though her pulse hadn't fully calmed. The adrenaline from the fight still surged through her, making her hyperaware of the quiet around them. The bodies of the four-man kill team were scattered across the forest floor, a reminder of how close they had come to losing.

Bishop wiped the remaining blood from his face, casting a glance at Hatch. "We're not sticking around when they come looking for their boys," he muttered, his voice low but carrying an unspoken urgency. He was already calculating their next move.

Hatch didn't respond right away. Her hand went to the radio clipped to her belt, the one Sheriff Tuck had given her before everything had gone sideways. She was about to press the button when a crackle of static interrupted the silence.

"Shots fired. Multiple reports of automatic gunfire over the ridge."

Bishop's eyes flicked toward the radio, his expression hardening, but he remained silent. He shook his head, signaling it wasn't their concern.

"Not our problem," Bishop said. "Let's move."

But before they could take a step, another transmission came through, this one frantic and raw. Tuck's voice.

"Shots fired at the station... hostage situation..." His words were punctuated by ragged breathing, tension lacing every syllable. "Maggie... stay calm. I said drop the gun!"

Hatch froze. Her heart slammed in her chest as her eyes shot to Bishop. The desperation in the sheriff's voice hit her like a physical blow. Maggie was in danger.

"Looks like your second target's still on someone's agenda," Hatch said quietly, her voice tense with urgency.

Bishop's face darkened, his jaw clenching. "Crystal Springs doesn't leave loose ends."

"How far is the station?" she asked, already running through options in her mind.

"Too far to reach on foot in time," Bishop tapped his gimp leg, scanning the landscape with practiced eyes, looking for any possible advantage. His eyes narrowed as he spotted the ridge line overlooking the station. "But maybe we don't need to get there."

Hatch followed his line of sight. She could see the faint outline of the station's roof, a distant dot through the trees.

Bishop's voice was calm, measured. "How fast does a bullet travel?"

She blinked, shifting gears as she realized what Bishop was implying. "Depends on the caliber and conditions."

"At this range, around 2,700 feet per second. I can make the shot from here with the right windage."

A thousand meters. Hatch's gut twisted. It was a long shot, but Bishop wasn't just any sniper. He'd clearly made shots like this before. But the distance, the conditions, the pressure—everything was stacked against them.

Her eyes narrowed as she studied the terrain. The ridge offered the perfect vantage point. It was high enough to give them a clear line of sight to the station. But something gnawed at her.

Bishop was already on the move, low and swift through the trees, leading the way to the ridge that overlooked the station. Hatch followed, her body moving automatically, her mind churning. This wasn't just about getting there. It was about making the shot.

They pushed through the dense forest, the climb steep and grueling.

Hatch could hear her own breath, sharp and controlled as she kept pace with Bishop. Every step was a battle against time. They had to get there before it was too late.

When they reached the top of the ridge, Bishop dropped to one knee, pulling the rifle from his rucksack, the same rifle he'd used to take out Sawyer. Hands moving with the fluidity of a trained professional, he assembled the rifle piece by piece. Suppressor, scope, stock—all clicking into place with mechanical precision.

Hatch crouched beside him, her eyes locking on the distant station. Processing the variables—distance, elevation, wind. She knew what needed to be done, but it wasn't going to be easy.

Bishop dropped to his belly, prone, settling into the familiar position of a sniper. His breathing slowed, the rifle becoming an extension of him. But something was wrong. His hands shook as he tried to steady the weapon, there was a slightly unfocused look to his eyes as he peered through the scope.

Bishop muttered, barely audible. "The toxin... it's still affecting my vision." His voice was steady, but she could hear the frustration beneath it. He was trying to shake it off, trying to push through the effects of Banyan's reagent that still clung to his system.

Hatch glanced at him, understanding the implications. Bishop was a master at this, but not today. Not like this.

Bishop's hands faltered again, his breathing uneven now. Hesitating, he pulled away from the scope, his jaw tight. "I can't make the shot."

Hatch nodded and slipped into position, as if the rifle had been hers all along. Bishop moved out of her way, staying low on the ground next to her. Her cheek pressed against the stock, eyes narrowing as she adjusted the scope. The station came into focus, just as Tuck's voice crackled through the radio again.

"Maggie—stay calm—"

There was no time to dwell on the stakes, no space for hesitation. The wind shifted—light, maybe two to three miles per hour—but enough to matter. She adjusted her holdover instinctively, compensating for the drift. Her mind ran the calculations in seconds: wind velocity, drop at range, target distance. The Coriolis effect barely registered, but she accounted for it anyway. Bishop watched her, his eyes still sharp despite the physical toll the dermal patch had taken. He didn't question her ability. In that moment, there was no room for doubt. Only precision.

"You've done this before," he said, his voice low, almost impressed.

Hatch's finger hovered just above the trigger, her breathing slowing as she steadied herself. "Not my first rodeo."

Exhaling slowly, feeling the weight of the rifle, the tension in her muscles coiled, ready. Her eyes locked on the target. Mind quiet now. One shot. One chance.

The wind brushed against her skin, and she adjusted once more. The distance didn't scare her. The shot didn't scare her. It was just a problem to be solved.

She felt the slight curvature of the trigger against the pad of her index finger. She inhaled, held the breath for a beat and then released it slowly. At the natural respiratory pause, Hatch slowly applied the pressure.

MAGGIE'S WORLD shrank to a single, terrifying point: the cold, unyielding pressure of the gun pressed against her temple. The hard metal dug into her skin, each tiny shift a brutal reminder of how close she was to death. Reeves' arm wrapped around her, tight and unforgiving, making it hard to breathe. Her heart pounded in her chest, the rhythm so frantic it drowned out everything else—the sounds of the rain, the voices of the deputies, even her own desperate thoughts.

This can't be happening. Please, God, don't let this be real.

Across the rain-soaked parking lot, Sheriff Tuck stood motionless, his gun raised, eyes locked on Reeves. His deputies were in position, their cars forming a loose perimeter, red and blue lights flashing against the wet pavement. But Reeves kept Maggie close, moving her with him each time an officer tried to flank them. He was in complete control.

"Nobody has to get hurt, Sheriff," Reeves said, his voice too calm. The drizzle softened his words but carried them clearly. "I'm walking out of here with Maggie. Once I'm clear, I'll let her go. Unharmed."

"He's lying, Sheriff! Don't let him—" The barrel pressed harder into her head, arm tighter around her throat, cutting off her words, her breath.

Tuck's eyes flicked to hers, fierce with determination. "That won't happen, Maggie. I promise."

Reeves chuckled, low and rough. "You have no idea who you're up against, Sheriff," he said, his tone casual but cold. "The people I work for will burn this place to the ground without thinking twice. Everyone in it. To get what they want." His grip tightened on her, fingers digging into her arm. "And what they want is her—and whatever's on that thumb drive."

Maggie's stomach turned, the weight of those words sinking in. This wasn't just about her anymore. These people had already taken everything—her father, Sawyer—and now they would take her. Terror spread through her, freezing her limbs, but she forced herself to focus on Tuck, silently begging him to do something.

A deputy's voice crackled over the radio. "No clean shot, sir."

Reeves shifted impatiently. "I'm getting tired of this dance, Sheriff. Hate for my finger to slip." His finger twitched on the trigger, the pressure on Maggie's head increasing. She could smell the gun oil, sharp and metallic. "Would be a shame. Can you live with that?"

Tuck didn't move. His jaw tightened, his knuckles white on the handle of his gun. A single drop of sweat slid down his nose, barely noticeable in the dim light. "Lower your weapon," he commanded, his voice steady, though Maggie could sense the strain in his words.

Reeves smirked, his voice smug. "Smart choice."

Maggie's heart raced faster, her breath coming in shallow, uneven bursts. Cold sweat ran down her back, mixing with the warm breath of Reeves on her neck. She tried to focus, but her world narrowed to one terrifying truth: Reeves' finger was too close to the trigger. Every tiny movement sent fear surging through her body. She squeezed her eyes shut, silently praying.

Please, Sheriff ... do something.

The moments dragged on, each one heavier than the last. The gun pressed harder against her skin, the cold metal unyielding. The rain dripped steadily, soaking into her clothes, the smell of wet asphalt and gunpowder filling her lungs.

Then, a single gunshot shattered the night.

The sound hit her like a physical force, a burst of noise that drowned out everything. For an instant, everything stopped. Warmth splashed across her face, the pressure against her neck released. Maggie's eyes opened wide, her mind struggling to understand what had just happened. She blinked, her vision blurring, trying to make sense of the chaos.

The gun was gone. The cold pressure against her head vanished, and Reeves' grip loosened. His bodyweight slumped against her back, nearly toppling her over before falling away to the side.

Blood. It was everywhere, pooling around Reeves' head, mixing with the rainwater on the pavement. His eyes stared lifelessly at the sky, the back of his skull a ruin of blood and bone.

Maggie's breath caught in her throat. Her legs trembled, threatening to give way as the shock hit her. She stumbled, her body no longer her own, the world tilting. The blood on her face hot, real.

"Maggie!" Tuck's voice cut through the haze.

Strong arms caught her before she hit the ground. He pulled her back, away from the body, his grip steady, grounding her when everything else was spinning out of control.

She clung to him, her chest heaving as her breath came in shallow, ragged bursts. The adrenaline drained from her, leaving her weak and trembling. The fear, the relief, the shock—it all slammed into her at once, too much to process. Her body shook, tears stinging her eyes and sobs escaping her mouth.

"It's over," Tuck whispered, his voice firm but gentle, trying to calm her. "It's over. You're safe now."

The words felt distant, the weight of the moment still pressing down on her. Her vision blurred again, her body heavy as exhaustion took over. She barely registered Tuck holding her tighter, guiding her away from the grisly scene.

She was safe. But all she could feel was the blood on her face, the warmth slowly cooling as the rain washed it away.

THIRTY-EIGHT

HATCH STEADIED THE RIFLE. THROUGH THE SCOPE, THE CROSSHAIRS FIXED on Reeves' motionless body. Blood pooled beneath him, spreading out into the rain-soaked parking lot. The threat was gone. She let out a slow breath and stood, her muscles tight from the tension of the shot. As she rose, Bishop, still leaning on a nearby tree, gave her a long look.

"Hell of a shot," he muttered, his voice rough but laced with approval. He wiped a hand over his face, as if trying to clear away the lingering effects of the dermal patch.

The silence after the gunshot weighed heavy, but not for long.

Bishop straightened, his eyes narrowing as he glanced back toward the bodies of the kill squad scattered around them. "I'm supposed to be dead, and as far as they know, you are, too." He shifted his stance, still visibly worn from the aftereffects of the toxin. "And Thorne hasn't checked in since they called for that clean slate order. General's expecting an update."

Hatch furrowed her brow. They had a short window before Delta 6 would start asking questions. If the General found out the kill squad had failed, they wouldn't have time to escape.

"We need to buy ourselves some breathing room," she said, more to herself than to Bishop.

Bishop looked to the ground, where Stone's gear lay in a heap. He knelt down and picked up the comms set. "We can use this." He adjusted the settings on the device, turning the earpiece over in his hands. "I'll pose as Stone. Contact Thorne, tell them Hatch is neutralized, and we're cleaning up."

Hatch frowned but quickly saw the logic. "You're sure that'll hold?"

Bishop looked up, eyes sharp despite his weakened state. "It'll hold long enough for us to disappear. But we need to make it look good."

Without waiting for her response, Bishop adjusted the mic and clipped it to his jacket. His voice changed, shifting into Stone's cold, commanding tone. "This is Stone. Hatch is down. No need for extraction. We'll handle cleanup."

"Nice work, Bishop. When you're done playing assassin, maybe try your hand at ventriloquism. You've got the voice thing down."

For a moment, there was only static. Hatch felt the pressure build in her chest, the uncertainty hanging in the air. Then, the reply came. "Copy that. Report back once all loose ends are tied. You're on your own until then."

Bishop cut the comms and stood. "That'll buy us time."

Hatch didn't relax at that, her mind already working on the next part of the plan. They couldn't rely on that lie holding forever.

"We still need to deal with the locals," she said, reaching into her jacket for her encrypted phone. She dialed quickly, the familiar sound of Tracy's voice cutting through the static.

"Glad to hear you're alive. And Bishop?"

"He's with me," she said. "There'll be time for explaining later. As far as Thorne knows, we're both dead."

"Nothing like dumping a burning bag of crap on my doorstep."

"Need a favor."

"Okay, shoot."

"We've got to clean things up here a bit. Thorne's little kill squad is down. I'm going to need you to run some interference with the local sheriff. Just long enough to clear my trail until I can set things right with Thorne."

"Not sure I understand everything at play here."

"Might be best you don't. At least for the time being." Hatch paused, knowing the position she was putting him in. "I know what I'm asking is a lot. And I wouldn't be if there was any other way around it. Right now, I don't think there is."

"Tell me what you can, and I'll do my part."

Hatch gave a rapid-fire sequence of events, culminating with the shot she took to neutralize Reeves.

Tracy let out a low whistle. "This is a tall order."

"I need forty-eight hours," she said.

Before Tracy could respond, another voice joined the line, laced with sarcasm. Banyan. "We've got you covered."

"That's the plan." Hatch eyed Bishop. "And by the way, that dermal patch really saved our asses here. You're a miracle worker."

"I'll take my bow when you're back here in one piece."

Tracy's voice returned, more serious now. "Alright, I'll buy you the time you need. I'll make arrangements. The General's not going to sit still for long."

"See you then." Hatch ended the call.

She looked on as Bishop disassembled his sniper rifle. The tension of their previous standoff settled, but there was still an undercurrent of things left unsaid. As the last click of metal echoed, Bishop looked up, his eyes catching Hatch's.

"I don't normally make it a habit of talking about past actions. Not my way, but—" He cleared his throat. "A while back I was tasked to support a cleanup op. Target was the daughter of a former Talon operator. One of the original members. She'd been kicking the hornet's nest for a while, stirring things up." He paused, watching for a reaction, but Hatch remained stone-faced.

"They sent a team. The team got wiped out, but not before she was killed. Or that's what they said." Bishop wiped his hand across his mouth, looking away. "Then I heard another rumor. She didn't die. She survived and ended up becoming part of Talon herself." He looked directly at her now. "Sound familiar?"

Hatch raised an eyebrow. Her response came dry, calm. "Vaguely."

"You're a strange duck." Bishop shook his head. "So why join Talon? After all that?"

Hatch's eyes drifted to the horizon, where the outline of Pinewood Falls was just barely visible through the haze of rain and fog. "You know the saying—keep your enemies closer." She paused, turning back to Bishop. "Plus, I figured I'd pick up where my dad left off."

"Following someone else's footsteps can lead you off a cliff."

"Yet I'm still walking."

"Tough way to live, though." Bishop hesitated, the tension returning to his face. "Tracy's a good man, but there are things he's not privy to."

"What are you getting at?"

Bishop took a breath before responding. "Thorne gave the order. He called me off, said you'd been taken care of. Guess I'm not the only one who's got experience playing dead?"

Hatch thought back to those desperate moments inside her family's home, back in Colorado. It seemed like a lifetime ago. To the world, both she and Nighthawk died that night. Cruise had brought her back. He convinced her to take the leap. To join Talon, the same group who'd been responsible for her father's death. The group who tried and failed to do the same to her. Now she stood at the crossroads once again.

"If it's any consolation, I doubt Tracy ever knew. He probably did think it was over."

"Whoever brought you onboard made a smart move. Working for them made it harder for him to finish you off."

She thought of Cruise. Maybe he'd suspected it all along. Maybe that's why he'd brought her onboard. Kept her close, the best way he could think of to keep her safe.

"Thorne's no slouch," Bishop continued. "He's a tactician. Just needed to wait for the opportunity."

"And he saw it here."

"Genius, when you think about it. Well, evil genius, but genius all the same. I take out Sawyer. You take me out. Bring in a team to finish the job. And the slate is wiped clean. You, the casualty of war and I the patsy."

The puzzle now made sense. Thorne had orchestrated everything, using Talon as both her shield and her downfall. She'd been a walking target for how long? Would it ever end?

Bishop's voice broke the silence. "Now you know."

Hatch stood there for a moment, processing. "Yeah. Now I know."

"The real question is, what do you plan to do about it?"

"The thing I'm best at."

They both stood in silence, the quiet of the forest returning as the weight of everything settled between them. Bishop's tone shifted. "Look, I'm going off the grid for a while. Too exposed for the time being. Need to make sure the trail's clear before I surface again."

"Smart move. Stay off the radar until it's safe."

There was a brief pause before Bishop spoke again, more hesitant this time. "I've got one last favor to ask. I know I don't deserve it, but it's something I need."

Hatch crossed her arms, listening.

"My sister lives in a small town in Texas—Riverton. Not much there but dust and oil fields." His voice softened. "She's got a daughter, my niece. Just turned ten." He swallowed, the words heavier than before. "I love that kid more than anything. I can't reach out to them. Not yet. Not 'til it's safe. But they need to know I'm alive. It'd kill her if they thought I was killed."

Hatch's face remained unreadable, but she understood the request. She'd been through this before, distancing herself from her niece and nephew to keep them safe. "You want me to tell them?"

Bishop pleaded with his eyes, but his words remained steady. "If you could. Just to let them know I'll come back when it's safe. They're good people. They're the best part of me."

Hatch considered for a moment. *Good people.* No escaping the code. And without a trace of doubt, if the tables were turned, he would do the same for her.

She gave a slow nod. "I'll do it."

Relief flickered across Bishop's face. "Riverton, Texas. Small place. You'll find them easy enough." He pulled a small writing pad from his pack and jotted down the address.

Hatch took it. A smudge of blood marked the corner of the paper. "I'll make sure they know."

"Thanks." He finished packing up his gear, snapping the case shut before standing to face her.

Hatch's expression softened just a fraction, and with a dry smile, she said, "Thanks for dying for me."

Bishop chuckled, a real laugh this time. "Who knew death could be so liberating?"

They stood for a moment longer, the silence no longer uncomfortable. Then, with one last look, Bishop slung his bag over his shoulder and disappeared into the woods, his figure quickly swallowed by the trees.

Hatch watched him go, standing still for a moment, her thoughts turning back to what lay ahead. Her path was set to Coronado, and not to take orders. Now, Hatch was walking back into Thorne's world with a plan of her own.

He wanted a clean slate. I'll show him what that means.

THIRTY-NINE

THE SCENE OUTSIDE THE SHERIFF'S STATION BUZZED WITH QUIET URGENCY. Voices murmured between the deputies as they moved with purpose, coordinating the aftermath. Yellow tape stretched along the edges of the chaos, marking out boundaries that were invisible to Hatch as she walked through the scene.

She passed through unnoticed, although the weight of everything hung over her. Her eyes scanned the crowd, settling on Maggie, wrapped in a blanket on the bumper of an ambulance. A paramedic checked her vitals, his voice soft and reassuring. Maggie's eyes were distant, her face pale and glassy, as if she was still trying to process the nightmare she had narrowly escaped.

Hatch approached slowly, her boots crunching softly against the gravel. As she neared, Maggie's head lifted, her eyes blinking back into focus. Looking fragile, as though the wind had knocked her down, she barely found the strength to stand again.

"They won't be coming after you," Hatch said quietly, crouching beside her. Her voice was low, meant only for Maggie. "It's over. Whatever's on that drive of yours, it'll bury the people responsible."

Maggie stared at her, the words sinking in slowly, her brow creasing in confusion. "Who ... who are you?"

"Just someone who happened to be in the right place at the right time."

Maggie let out a small, breathless laugh. "If this is the right place, I'd hate to see the wrong one."

"It's all a matter of perspective."

Standing up, she felt the strain of the day in her muscles. The girl was alive, and for now, that was enough.

Hatch moved with purpose. Sheriff Tuck stood just inside the station doors, overseeing the remnants of the chaos. When their eyes met, Tuck raised his brows in silent acknowledgment, then followed Hatch's gesture, stepping aside into a quieter corner of the room.

"I cleaned up most of the mess on the hill," Hatch said in a low voice, speaking only for him. "Someone from my agency will contact you soon, give you the spin. You'll know what to say by then."

Tuck's eyes flicked toward the body under the bloodstained sheet nearby—the remains of Reeves. "Hell of a shot." He shook his head, frustration lining his face. "You wouldn't know anything about that, would you?"

Hatch's lips curled into the hint of a smirk, but her eyes stayed cold. "I didn't take the shot, Sheriff. You did. Remember?" She leaned in slightly, her voice barely above a whisper. "I'm dead. Ghosts don't pull triggers."

Tuck chuckled under his breath, but the weariness never left his expression. His eyes shifted, searching her face for something deeper. "And that guy we were after ... the one who started all of this?"

Hatch's expression darkened, her tone firm. "He won't be a problem anymore."

Tuck studied her, a question hanging on the tip of his tongue. After a moment, he seemed to think better of it, simply accepting her answer without pressing for more. They stood in silence for a beat, the air heavy with unspoken words.

Tuck cleared his throat. "Gonna take a while for things to feel normal around here."

Hatch looked at him, a flicker of amusement in her eyes. "Normal's overrated." She let the words settle between them, a quiet truth they both understood.

Tuck's weariness was clearly etched in his expression. "You need a ride back to your motel? I can at least do that much."

Hatch shook her head, glancing at the clouds that were finally beginning to break, slivers of sunlight pushing through. "You've got your hands full here, Sheriff." She made her way back to the doors, glancing back at him. "Besides, the walk will do me some good."

Tuck studied her for a moment, something unspoken lingering between them. "Take care of yourself, Hatch."

Already turning away, her boots crunched softly against the gravel as she walked down the road, her back straight, her steps measured. She didn't look back as the station faded behind her, the slivers of sunlight growing brighter as the clouds continued to part.

Ahead of her was the next fight. There was always another mess to clean up. Somewhere down the road, she'd find it.

FORTY

THE LOBBY OF THE HOTEL DEL CORONADO WAS ALIVE WITH UNDERSTATED luxury. Soft conversations floated beneath the high ceilings, where chandeliers cast a warm, golden light across the marble floors. The ocean's distant rumble mixed with the clinking of glasses from the nearby bar. It was a place designed to soothe, to make you forget about anything beyond the serene elegance of the moment. But for Hatch, there was no forgetting what lay behind.

She moved through the space quietly. The familiar surroundings did nothing to calm her. The hotel had always been a backdrop to another life—one that seemed far removed from the weight she now carried. Tonight, it was the setting for something darker.

In a quiet corner, near the edge of the lobby, Banyan was waiting. Sitting casually in one of the oversized chairs, his posture relaxed, his eyes were sharp, tracking her every movement. His usual smirk was in place, but there was something more behind it—a knowing, a readiness.

As she reached him, there was no need for pleasantries. Their history filled in the gaps of what didn't need to be said.

Glancing around, his tone carrying a quiet amusement. "The past sure has a way of sticking to you."

Hatch didn't respond right away. She lowered herself into the seat

across from him. The moment stretched out as the atmosphere around them buzzed with the hotel's quiet opulence. But the tension between them was palpable.

Banyan leaned in slightly, his voice dropping. "Are you sure about this?" It wasn't an accusation, but there was caution there—a man who knew just how deep things were about to go.

Hatch's reply was calm, almost detached. "I always am."

Banyan reached into his jacket. He pulled out a transdermal patch, identical to the one he'd given her before. He held it out in his open palm. His voice was softer now. "He made a mistake putting crosshairs on you," he said. "I just want to make sure you don't end up in them again."

Hatch reached for the patch, her fingers brushing lightly against the vial before she slipped both into her pocket. The weight of the moment sat between them, heavy and unspoken.

"No trace?" she asked, her voice quiet, but carrying an edge of urgency. She didn't need details, just confirmation.

Banyan leaned back slightly, the smirk returning to his face, but it didn't touch his eyes. "None that any lab will find." His response was quick, certain. He'd done this before.

Hatch accepted the answer without a second thought. She didn't need more than that. There was a finality to what came next, and the fewer questions, the cleaner it would be.

For a moment, there was silence. The hum of the hotel lobby drifted back in, the faint sounds of distant conversations reminding them they were surrounded by people completely unaware of the gravity of the exchange.

"I'm indebted to you," Hatch said, her voice softer now. It wasn't something she said lightly, but it was true. Banyan had been there for her more times than she could count.

Banyan leaned back further in his chair. "You paid your debt in full a long time ago." But beneath his casual tone, there was a truth they both understood. Their lives had crossed too many times for any score to need to be settled. It was a constant, shifting balance.

Hatch accepted his words. There was no need for elaboration. It was just how things were between them.

Banyan studied her for a moment longer, then spoke, his voice lowering once again. "So, what's next?" The question was more a formality than anything else. He knew better than to expect a full answer.

Hatch shrugged slightly, her expression still unreadable. "Just cleaning up loose ends."

Banyan chuckled, the sound more resigned than amused. "Loose ends have a way of tightening up if you let them sit too long. Be careful."

Hatch stood up. "Always."

Turning, she walked away from the quiet corner of the lobby, her path set. Banyan watched her go, his easy smirk slipping as she disappeared into the crowd. He knew better than anyone that Hatch didn't leave things unfinished.

Outside, the cool night air greeted her, and the faint rumble of the ocean broke the silence.

FORTY-ONE

BEAUREGARD COVINGTON PACED THE LENGTH OF HIS BEDROOM, HIS breath coming in shallow bursts. His movements were frantic, tossing clothes into the open suitcase without care. Each shirt he threw in seemed to make his hands shake more. The phone pressed to his ear felt like an anchor pulling him under, its weight dragging his anxiety deeper. On the other end of the line, Ambrose's voice was low and lethal, each word landing like a blow.

"This town isn't worth the trouble," Covington spat, his voice thick with fear. "It's falling apart, and when it goes down, everyone's going down with it. I'm not staying here to be buried with them."

Silence greeted him on the other end, Ambrose's lack of response more menacing than any threat. Finally, his voice came through cold and final. "No one fails me. You think you can just walk away? You're part of this, whether you like it or not."

Covington stopped packing for a moment, sweat beading on his brow. His hand gripped the edge of the suitcase as he tried to steady himself. "It's only a matter of time before the story breaks. Crystal Springs, the senator—it's all going to blow up. And when it does, I'm not sticking around. I'm getting out before the feds swarm this place."

The silence on the line stretched again. Covington swallowed, his heart racing. He could hear Ambrose's slow, deliberate breath through the phone, and the weight of it made his stomach churn.

"Your name will be the first I drop when they ask who ran Pinewood Falls into the ground."

Covington let out a shaky laugh, but it sounded more like a desperate gasp. "Good luck finding me. I'll be long gone before it comes to that."

Disconnecting the call before Ambrose could respond, he dropped the phone on the bed with a muted thud. For a moment, the silence in the room was a relief. He stood there, breathing heavily, staring at the mess of clothes in the suitcase as if it held some answer he couldn't see.

"Goddamn psychopath," he muttered, zipping up the suitcase with trembling hands. He turned toward the door and called out, "Daryl! Get up here and help with these bags!"

Silence.

Covington's brow furrowed. "Daryl!" he shouted louder, his frustration rising with each unanswered call. He stormed out of the bedroom, his heart thudding in his chest as he stepped into the hallway. "You useless—"

The words caught in his throat.

Daryl, his trusted enforcer, lay slumped against the wall, his lifeless eyes staring into nothing. A dark pool of blood had spread beneath him, glistening in the dim light. For a moment, Covington couldn't move. The world narrowed to that single horrific image—the man who was supposed to protect him, crumpled and dead.

His breath hitched, panic seizing him. His feet stumbled backward, but before he could fully process the shock, a figure emerged from the shadows at the end of the hall.

Bishop.

Covington's legs buckled, and he collided with the doorframe. His wide, terrified eyes locked onto Bishop's, calm and cold, like death itself.

"Bishop ..." Covington's voice was barely a whisper. Taking a shaky step backward, desperation crept into his words. "I I can pay you. Whatever Ambrose is giving you, I'll double it. Triple it, even."

Bishop didn't respond immediately. His face was unreadable, his eyes fixed on Covington without a hint of emotion. He stepped forward slowly, each movement deliberate, as if giving Covington time to squirm. The silence stretched, heavy and oppressive. When Bishop finally spoke, his voice was low, final. "This one's pro bono."

Panic erupted in Covington's chest. He scrambled backward, tripping over his own feet as he fell onto the bed. His hands fumbled, reaching for something—anything—to protect himself, but there was nothing. "Please," he begged, his voice rising in desperation. "Please, I can help you. We can—"

The last word died on his lips.

Bishop raised the pistol, the sleek black suppressor catching the dim light as he took aim. His finger squeezed the trigger.

A single shot.

The muted pop of the silencer was almost anticlimactic. Covington's body jerked, a crimson bloom spreading across his chest. His eyes went wide in shock, mouth open as he gasped his final breath. Blood trickled from his lips, staining the front of his once-pristine shirt. His body slumped forward, lifeless.

Bishop holstered the gun, his expression unchanged. Without a second glance, he stepped over the fallen man, his boots silently leaving even prints across the floor. The silence of the house enveloped him as he made his way toward the door, the wind outside carrying the faint sound of rustling leaves as if the world had already moved on.

Another loose end tied.

FORTY-TWO

THE FOLLOWING MORNING, GENERAL THORNE SAT AT HIS DESK, THE QUIET hum of his office a stark contrast to the turmoil brewing in his mind. Finger tapping impatiently on his phone screen, he tried, for the third time, to reach Stone. Nothing. The silence on the other end of the line was beginning to wear on him. Stone hadn't checked in, and the kill team was MIA.

His jaw tightened. Accustomed to control, to orchestrating events from afar, now something was slipping. The usual satisfaction he found in reading the headlines about the fallout from Pinewood Falls couldn't distract him from the gnawing doubt creeping into his thoughts.

The door swung open, abruptly interrupting his moment of reflection. Thorne's head jerked up, and the faint irritation on his face gave way to shock.

Hatch stood in the doorway, her silhouette sharp and confident. There was no hesitation in her movement as she stepped inside, the door clicking shut behind her.

For a second, Thorne froze, his mind scrambling to make sense of her presence. "Hatch?" His voice was strained. He failed to mask the confusion. "Thank God, you're alive! We thought—"

"You won't be able to reach him." She stepped further into the room. "Stone's out of the game."

Thorne blinked, the words sinking in. He faltered. "Stone? I—"

"Save it," Hatch said, her voice sharp. She crossed the room in a few measured steps, coming to a stop in front of his desk. "I know everything. The hit on Sawyer. The plan to silence Maggie. The kill team you sent to clean it all up."

Thorne stood slowly, trying to compose himself, but the shock hadn't fully left his face. His hand rested on the back of his chair, as if steadying himself. "I ... I was briefed by Tracy," he began, his tone careful. "I was told Stone's team engaged Bishop. It appears the team was killed in the exchange."

Hatch's eyes narrowed. "And since I'm standing here, alive, you're wondering if Bishop is, too."

Thorne hesitated, his mouth opening slightly before he closed it again. Clearing his throat, he attempted to regain control. "Hatch, you have to understand—this was never personal. You weren't the target. Things escalated. You know how these operations go."

"I know men like you, Thorne. Men who think they can move their people like pieces on a chessboard. Sacrifice here, manipulate there, all for the endgame." Hatch took a step closer, her eyes locking onto his. "I'm not a pawn. Never was."

Thorne raised his hands, placating, but the tension in his jaw betrayed him. "You were never a pawn, Hatch. I—"

"I'm done with Talon. You don't come after me, and I won't expose your little arrangement with Crystal Springs and the senator. We call it a truce."

There was a flicker of something in Thorne's eyes—calculation, a momentary pause as he weighed his options. The silence stretched as his mind worked. "Of course. No one will come after you. You have my word. We can move on from this. You've proven yourself to be a true asset."

Hatch read the lie in his expression as easily as if he'd spoken it aloud. But she didn't react, didn't give him the satisfaction of knowing she'd caught it. Instead, she stepped forward, extending her hand. "A promise is only as good as the hand that shakes on it. Something my dad used to say."

Thorne eyed her hand, suspicion darkening his features, but he couldn't afford to refuse. Slowly, he reached out, his grip firm, almost as if trying to reassert control. "You remind me a lot of him."

The moment their hands touched, Hatch pressed her thumb against the small dermal patch hidden in her palm. A soft, almost imperceptible pop followed. Thorne struggled to release his hand. Hatch held it a moment longer, wanting to ensure the venom found its mark.

He pulled his hand back, glancing down at it. His eyes already had begun glossing over. "What the hell...?"

"You made a mistake. A fatal one." Hatch's expression didn't change. "I'm no pawn. I'm the queen. And this is checkmate."

Thorne's face contorted in sudden realization. His hand flew to his chest as his heart rate began to spike erratically. Panic flashed in his eyes as his body started to fail him. He staggered backward, reaching for the edge of the desk, but his legs buckled. His breath came in shallow gasps, his hand trembling as it moved toward his phone.

He never made it.

Fingers twitching uselessly, his heart faltered and then stopped altogether. His body slumped into the chair, lifeless, his eyes wide with the terror of his final moments.

Hatch stood there for a beat across from Thorne's corpse. No emotion crossed her face. No second thoughts. She turned on her heel, walking toward the door, the soft click of the handle punctuating the silence in the room as she left.

FORTY-THREE

THE SETTING SUN PAINTED PINEWOOD FALLS IN HUES OF FIRE AND GOLD, casting long shadows across Main Street like accusations laid bare. Sheriff Roy Tuck stood on the weathered porch of Evelyn Hartwell's home, his hat a dead weight in his hands. The pistol at his hip felt heavier than it had in years, a constant reminder of just how close she'd come to death.

Inside, the soft hum of the television barely masked the tension hanging in the air. Tuck lowered himself onto the worn leather couch beside Evelyn, the cushions creaking beneath his weight. Her hand found his knee—warm, steady, grounding him in a way nothing else could.

The news broadcast flickered to life, bathing the dim room in a cold, blue glow. Aerial shots of Pinewood Falls filled the screen, familiar streets now foreign under the harsh glare of media scrutiny.

The anchor's voice cut through the silence, sharp and clinical. "Breaking news from Pinewood Falls. The investigation into Crystal Springs has uncovered a web of corruption and violence that has shaken this small town to its core."

Tuck's jaw clenched, his stubbled face tight with the weight of everything. His town. His responsibility. Now stripped bare for the world to see.

"Authorities have confirmed the discovery of Malcolm Trent's body at the bottom of his well. His death is the latest linked to the unfolding scandal, just days after the shooting death of Nathan Sawyer, which investigators now believe was intentional and directly tied to Senator Masterson's involvement with the megacorporation Crystal Springs. The senator and his associates are facing charges for illegal land grabs, conspiracy, and intimidation tactics."

Tuck's fingers twitched, the muscle memory of reaching for his notepad instinctual, even though there was nothing left to write down. He watched, heart heavy, as the camera panned across the streets he'd walked a thousand times. The same streets he'd sworn to protect, now tainted beyond recognition.

"CEO of Crystal Springs, Jason Ambrose, could not be reached for comment. Additional documents provided by an anonymous whistle-blower link the company to several deaths, including that of Malcolm Trent. Senator Masterson is expected to face charges, and further names are likely to be revealed as the investigation deepens."

Tuck exhaled slowly. He looked out the window, half-expecting to see news vans parked outside. The crickets were the only sound filling the night, as if the world had already moved on, leaving Pinewood Falls in the aftermath.

"The quiet town of Pinewood Falls—once known for its charm—faces a long road to recovery. With the story still unfolding, this community will need time to heal from its darkest chapter."

The remote was cold in Tuck's hand as he clicked off the TV, silence rushing in to fill the void. For a moment, he just sat there, the weight of it all pressing down on him.

"Guess that's our new claim to fame," Tuck muttered, his voice rough like sandpaper. He turned to Evelyn, the lines around his eyes deepening, the weariness catching up with him. "You sure you still want to stick around for the cleanup?"

Evelyn's fingers tightened on his knee. She looked into his eyes. Her quiet determination and strength reminded Tuck why he'd always been drawn to her.

"Roy Tuck, if you think I'm going anywhere, you've taken one too many knocks to the head."

A chuckle escaped him, rusty and unexpected, breaking through the tension that had wrapped itself around his chest for days. "Yes ma'am."

Evelyn leaned in closer, her lips brushing his cheek, the faint scent of lavender wrapping around him—a comforting reminder of quieter days, simpler times.

"We'll get through this," she whispered, her voice soft but certain. "Together."

Tuck released a breath he felt like he'd been holding for days. His arm slipped around her waist, pulling her in closer, letting her warmth seep into him.

For a while, they sat there in silence, the weight of the past few days slowly ebbing away. But as Tuck stared at the now-darkened TV, one thought lingered in his mind.

"She's one brave woman," he said quietly, his voice softer now. "Maggie's got that stubborn streak, just like her old man. Malcolm would've been proud of her, standing up like that."

Evelyn squeezed his hand, her head resting against his shoulder. "He would've. She did what needed to be done."

The heaviness in his chest lightened just a little more. They had weathered the storm, but the long road to recovery stretched out before them.

Outside, the last rays of sunlight dipped below the horizon, plunging Pinewood Falls into twilight. But here, in this moment, there was the faintest stirring of hope. Together, they would rebuild. One piece at a time.

FORTY-FOUR

THE COFFEE SHOP WAS QUIET, ITS WALLS BATHED IN SOFT MORNING LIGHT filtering through the large windows. The gentle hum of conversation from a few scattered patrons mixed with the sound of clinking cups and the distant crash of waves from the nearby coast. It was a far cry from the cold, sterile environments Hatch had grown accustomed to during her time with Talon. This place felt warmer, more real.

Hatch sat in the corner, her back to the wall, a steaming cup of black coffee in front of her. She hadn't touched it. Across from her, Tracy and Banyan were seated, the weight of their shared history palpable in the silence between them.

Tracy was the first to speak, his voice low but steady. "You're free and clear, Hatch. The situation with Thorne—it's never going to come back to haunt you. I've made sure of it."

Hatch studied him for a moment, her expression guarded. "That's what they said the first time someone put a target on my back."

Tracy didn't flinch. "I get it. But this time, it's different. Thorne was the one pulling the strings. With him gone, no one's left to come after you."

Hatch leaned back in her chair. "Talon hasn't felt like home since—" She stumbled over the words. "Ever since Cruise died, it's been off balance. And Thorne's involvement... well, that was the final nail in the coffin."

Banyan shifted, trying to lighten the mood. "You've got a knack for surviving, though. You've been a pain in a lot of people's asses, and yet, here you are."

Hatch allowed herself a small smirk, but it didn't quite reach her eyes. "I'm not giving them a third chance," she said, her voice firm. "I can't stay tied to this. Not anymore."

The air between them grew heavier as Tracy and Banyan exchanged glances. There was no sugarcoating it. Hatch was done. The decision was final.

Tracy's voice conveyed his understanding. "We won't try to convince you otherwise. You've earned that. And we'll always keep an ear out. If there's any whisper of trouble, you'll be the first to know."

Banyan leaned forward, his tone more serious than usual. "You know, the threat might not ever completely disappear. You've pissed off a lot of the wrong people." His attempt at humor was thin, but it showed his concern.

Hatch met his eyes. "I'm laying low for a while," she said, her tone even. "I need to keep my head down until I'm sure there's no lingering threat. Steering clear of my family until I know they won't get caught in the crossfire."

Tracy shifted, the conversation moving to practical matters. "We've set up an offshore account for you. Clean and untraceable. Banyan made sure of that. Consider it a severance package."

Hatch raised an eyebrow, half-amused. "Severance, huh? Didn't think I was entitled to one."

Tracy shrugged, his face serious. "You've done more for this organization than most people will ever know. Consider it a thank you."

"It's all set." Banyan tapped on his tablet, pulling up the details. "No one will be able to link it to you. You're basically a ghost now."

Hatch appreciated the gesture even though she knew it wasn't about the money. It never had been. "Thanks," she said quietly. "But this isn't about money. It's about freedom."

Both men fell silent, knowing there wasn't much left to say. They'd seen her through countless missions, countless near-death situations. And now, they were watching her walk away from it all.

"So," Tracy said, his voice quieter now, almost cautious. "What's next for you? Where do you go from here?"

Hatch's thoughts wandered to the mountains, to the promise she'd made to a man who was supposed to be dead. "I made a promise. And I plan to keep it."

Banyan's usual cocky demeanor softened, if only for a moment. "Wherever you go, Hatch, they won't forget you. But we'll always have your back."

Hatch finished her cup in a shared silence before standing. The weight of Talon, of Thorne, of everything that had led her to this point began to lift, if only slightly. She looked at the two men, both of whom had been by her side more times than she could count. She'd cut her own path before. She'd do it again.

"You take care of yourselves," she said, her tone a mix of gratitude and warning. "Don't get tangled up in anything you can't walk away from."

"Same goes for you."

Without another word, Hatch turned and headed for the door, her footsteps steady and purposeful. The cool morning air greeted her as she stepped outside. The fresh scent of the ocean carried on the breeze. The sun was rising higher, casting long shadows on the sidewalk as people passed by, oblivious to the world Hatch had just walked away from.

The future stretched out before her like an open road—uncertain, but free.

There was one thing she knew for sure.

There was a promise to keep. And Hatch always kept her promises.

Rachel Hatch's story continues in MIRAGE. Order here: https://www.amazon.com/dp/B0CXH5562Z

In a town where nothing is as it seems, survival is more than a mirage.

Rachel Hatch never breaks a promise. After a vow made during her last mission with Talon, she heads to the small, unassuming town of Riverton, Texas. But what should have been a simple visit quickly turns dark when a mysterious power outage plunges the town into isolation. As supplies dwindle and tempers flare, it becomes clear that Riverton isn't just dealing with a disaster—it's part of something far more sinister.

Hatch soon uncovers a secret buried beneath the town's surface: a chilling experiment designed to push the limits of human endurance. But as she digs deeper, she realizes the stakes are even higher—a dangerous military weapon system is being tested, with the town's unsuspecting residents as its pawns.

With the clock ticking and the town unraveling into chaos, Hatch must expose the truth and stop the experiment before Riverton becomes a battlefield. But in a world of shadows and deception, not everything is as it seems—and survival may demand sacrifices Hatch never anticipated.

Mirage is a high-octane thriller where loyalty, survival, and betrayal blur in a deadly game of cat and mouse.

https://www.amazon.com/dp/B0CXH5562Z

Join the LT Ryan reader family & receive a free copy of the Rachel Hatch story, *Fractured*. Click the link below to get started: https://ltryan.com/rachel-hatch-newsletter-signup-1

THE RACHEL HATCH SERIES

Drift

Downburst

Fever Burn

Smoke Signal

Firewalk

Whitewater

Aftershock

Whirlwind

Tsunami

Fastrope

Sidewinder

RACHEL HATCH SHORT STORIES

Fractured

Proving Ground

The Gauntlet

Join the LT Ryan reader family & receive a free copy of the Rachel Hatch story, Fractured. Click the link below to get started:

https://ltryan.com/rachel-hatch-newsletter-signup-1

Get your very own Rachel Hatch merchandise today! Click the link below to find coffee mugs, t-shirts, and even signed copies of your favorite L.T. Ryan thrillers! https://ltryan.ink/EvG_

ALSO BY L.T. RYAN

Find All of L.T. Ryan's Books on Amazon Today!

The Jack Noble Series

The Recruit (free)

The First Deception (Prequel 1)

Noble Beginnings

A Deadly Distance

Ripple Effect (Bear Logan)

Thin Line

Noble Intentions

When Dead in Greece

Noble Retribution

Noble Betrayal

Never Go Home

Beyond Betrayal (Clarissa Abbot)

Noble Judgment

Never Cry Mercy

Deadline

End Game

Noble Ultimatum

Noble Legend

Noble Revenge

Never Look Back (Coming Soon)

Bear Logan Series

Ripple Effect

Blowback

Take Down

Deep State

Bear & Mandy Logan Series

Close to Home

Under the Surface

The Last Stop

Over the Edge

Between the Lies

Caught in the Web (Coming Soon)

Rachel Hatch Series

Drift

Downburst

Fever Burn

Smoke Signal

Firewalk

Whitewater

Aftershock

Whirlwind

Tsunami

Fastrope

Sidewinder

Mitch Tanner Series

The Depth of Darkness

Into The Darkness

Deliver Us From Darkness

Cassie Quinn Series

Path of Bones

Whisper of Bones

Symphony of Bones

Etched in Shadow

Concealed in Shadow

Betrayed in Shadow

Born from Ashes

Return to Ashes (Coming Soon)

Blake Brier Series

Unmasked

Unleashed

Uncharted

Drawpoint

Contrail

Detachment

Clear

Quarry (Coming Soon)

Dalton Savage Series

Savage Grounds

Scorched Earth

Cold Sky

The Frost Killer

Crimson Moon (Coming Soon)

Maddie Castle Series

The Handler

Tracking Justice

Hunting Grounds

Vanished Trails

Smoldering Lies (Coming Soon)

Affliction Z Series

Affliction Z: Patient Zero

Affliction Z: Abandoned Hope

Affliction Z: Descended in Blood

Affliction Z : Fractured Part 1

Affliction Z: Fractured Part 2 (Fall 2021)

ABOUT THE AUTHOR

L.T. Ryan is a *USA Today* and international bestselling author. The new age of publishing offered L.T. the opportunity to blend his passions for creating, marketing, and technology to reach audiences with his popular Jack Noble series.

Living in central Virginia with his wife, the youngest of his three daughters, and their three dogs, L.T. enjoys staring out his window at the trees and mountains while he should be writing, as well as reading, hiking, running, and playing with gadgets. See what he's up to at http://ltryan.com.

Social Medial Links:

- Facebook (L.T. Ryan): https://www.facebook.com/LTRyanAuthor

- Facebook (Jack Noble Page): https://www.facebook.com/JackNobleBooks/

- Twitter: https://twitter.com/LTRyanWrites

- Goodreads: http://www.goodreads.com/author/show/6151659.L_T_Ryan

Made in the USA
Las Vegas, NV
15 December 2024

14364725R00128